Suddenly, Cai was falling through icy snow instead of sky.

His fall slowed until he stopped, snow packed beneath him. He just lay there for a moment, trying to take in the fact that he was still alive. Finally, he tried to move—but he was trapped!

Cai began to panic. He squirmed and wormed around until he managed to get his hand to his face. He pushed the snow away from his eyes and mouth, but it didn't help. All he could see was white. Then more snow collapsed on him and he was no better off than when he'd started. He tried to stay calm and remember what he had learned about staying alive in an avalanche.

He heard a sound above him—a sound like digging. A rescue team! he thought. He tried to shout, but snow fell in his mouth, muffling his words.

There came a low rumble that shook the snow around him. The digging sound began anew. Suddenly, it occurred to Cai just who his rescuers most probably were. *Sabertooths!*

VISIT THE EXCITING WORLD OF

IN THESE BOOKS:

Windchaser by Scott Ciencin

River Quest by John Vornholt

Hatchling by Midori Snyder

Lost City by Scott Ciencin

Sabertooth Mountain by John Vornholt

AND COMING SOON:

Thunder Falls by Scott Ciencin

DINOTOPIA®
SABERTOOTH MOUNTAIN

by John Vornholt

BULLSEYE BOOKS

Random House 🏠 New York

For the Hirsen family:
Phyllis, Steve, Rachael, and Molly

Special thanks to James Gurney and Scott Usher

A BULLSEYE BOOK PUBLISHED BY RANDOM HOUSE, INC.

http://www.randomhouse.com/

Library of Congress Catalog Card Number: 96-67748
ISBN 0-679-88095-X
RL: 5.7

Printed in the United States of America 10 9 8 7 6 5 4 3 2

Cover illustration by Michael Welply

SABERTOOTH MOUNTAIN

Windy Point

Crystal Caverns

The Hatchery

Baz

Pooktook

Volcaneum

NORTHERN PLAINS

CRACKSHELL POINT

Cornucopia   Deep Lake
Treetown   Bent Root

Palongo River

Temple Ruins   BACKBONE MOUNTAINS

Rocky Pass

Prosperine

Sapphire Bay

Poseidos
(sunken)

RAINY
BASIN

Hadro
Swamp

Waterfall City

GREAT CANAL

SKY GALLEY CAVES

Tentpole of the Sky

Sculpted Cliffs

Sky City

Thermala

The Time Towers

FORBIDDEN MOUNTAINS

Canyon City

Ancient Gorge

Red Rapid
Canyon

The Sentinels

Pteros

Amu River

Warmwater
Bay

Culebra

OUTER ISLAND

GREAT DESERT

The Portal

Sauropolis

Dolphin Bay

Chandara

BLACKWOOD
FLATS

Dragonfly Coast

Cape Turtletail

CHAPTER 1

Cai wriggled around in his saddle, but his tailbone still ached. After six hours of nonstop riding, Fatpelt felt like a giant barrel beneath him. To make matters worse, the wet snow had turned the woolly mammoth's thick fur into smelly ropes.

Cai rode on, uncomfortable though he was, through the narrow, icy passes of Mammoth Trail. On either side of him, walls of rock jutted into the clouds and vanished. The only sound was the *squish, squish* of mammoth feet in the slushy snow, leaving plenty of room for thought.

Cai Rochelle had lived most of his life in Thermala. Thanks to the hot springs, Thermala was the warmest city in the mountain region of the island of Dinotopia. The springs kept the city warm enough for dinosaurs to live there. No dinosaurs went higher than Thermala—only big mammals and humans. Cai had always thought that the humans up there must be a little crazy to want to stay where it was so cold and uncivilized. Now he'd been there himself, to go to school,

1

and he *still* thought the humans were crazy to stay. Although he did wish he'd waited a few more months before quitting school because the mountain passes were in danger of avalanches in the early spring.

Cai thought grumpily about the school at the Tentpole of the Sky. He had wanted to go to the boys' school in Treetown, where most of his friends went. But, no, *Moraine* had gone to the Tentpole of the Sky. And *Moraine* was now a Habitat Partner of the mountain region. So off to the Tentpole of the Sky Cai had gone. It wasn't fair!

Cai looked ahead at Moraine and Bigtusk as they plowed a path in the snow for Fatpelt to follow. Moraine was twenty-eight, fifteen years older than Cai, which made her seem more like an aunt than a sister. Like their mother, she was tall, slim, and beautiful. She took being a Habitat Partner very seriously—as she should—but Cai doubted that she ever had any fun. Moraine's partner, Bigtusk, was simply the hugest mammoth Cai had ever seen. He also had a temper to match his size. Together these two worked to maintain a balance in the mountain region between the land and the creatures who lived there.

Cai sighed into the hood of his coat. He knew he should be grateful. Moraine and Bigtusk had made a special trip to fetch him from the Tentpole of the Sky. No one else would have made a journey at this time of year. Even Fatpelt, a friend of the Habitat Partners, was doing Cai a favor by carrying him. Instead of making him feel better, this thought made Cai angry again. People were always doing him favors, treating him like a child. He couldn't stand it anymore! He was tired of it!

"I want to stop!" Cai blurted out.

Fatpelt halted immediately and proceeded to attack an evergreen bush. She yanked it up by the roots with her trunk and ate it whole. Bigtusk stomped the snow and rumbled angrily.

Moraine turned to look at Cai. "You want to stop *again*? We just stopped an hour ago."

Cai crossed his arms. "I only want to stretch my legs. I'm not used to riding around on a mammoth—my legs hurt."

"We want to reach Sky City before nightfall," Moraine reminded him.

"*You* want to reach Sky City before nightfall," answered Cai, glaring. "I don't care."

Moraine frowned, and clouds of steam shot from her mouth as she spoke. "You don't care about anything, do you? Mom and Dad send you to the best school on the island, and you quit after half a year. Then you make me and Bigtusk drop everything we're doing to come and get you!"

"I didn't ask for you to come and get me. That was *your* decision."

"Right!" she snapped. "Next time, I'll just let you take Mammoth Trail by yourself. Keep riding—we've got to get to Sky City in time for you to catch the sky galley."

"I don't want to go to Sauropolis either," he declared with a scowl. "I want to go home—to Thermala."

Moraine's jaw tightened. "Mom and Dad are in Sauropolis, so that's where you're going. I'm sorry, Cai, but the world does not revolve around you."

"That's for sure," muttered the boy. "I never get what I want. I wanted to go to school in Treetown. I've never seen Treetown, and I've seen the mountains all my life."

Moraine looked at Cai closely and her expression softened a little. "Okay, Little Brother, maybe you'll get your way. But first you're going to Sauropolis to explain to Mom and Dad why you quit school. You can't get out of that."

"Okay," said Cai glumly. Sometimes it felt as if he were all alone in the world. His sister had Bigtusk and her duties as Habitat Partner. His parents had each other and important jobs as surveyors, which kept them traveling all over the island. He had nobody.

Bigtusk grunted and plowed ahead. Beneath Cai, Fatpelt shook herself like a gigantic dog. Then she trotted after the other mammoth, bouncing Cai on his sore posterior.

"Do you have to make it worse?" shouted Cai.

Fatpelt made a sound that might have been a laugh. But she slowed down to her regular pace.

They rode for an hour more, until Bigtusk suddenly stopped. Then he snorted and pointed his trunk down the trail. Cai peered into the snowy gloom of the mountain pass, but he couldn't see anything.

Bigtusk trumpeted. A moment later, an answering call came from far off.

"You may get your chance to rest," said Moraine. "There's a caravan at the crossroads. We'll stop to talk with them, but just for a few minutes."

They wound their way through the gentle snowfall. The wind shifted, and Cai smelled the caravan ahead of them on the trail. There must be a lot of mammals, he thought, or maybe just a few that smelled especially bad. Fatpelt smelled them, too, and snorted through her trunk.

Finally they reached Daylight Pass, where Bison Trail intersected Mammoth to form a crossroads. Bison Trail headed west to the grazing land, and east into the wilderness of the Forbidden Mountains. The crossroads was one of the few places where you could see the sun over the peaks.

As they drew near the caravan, Cai's mouth dropped open. He had never seen so many different kinds of mammals together: woolly rhinoceroses, elks with giant antlers, hulking ground sloths, long-necked camels, bisons, mastodons, and a dozen other species. He guessed there were about forty animals in all.

The lad was thrilled at the sight of so many different mammals, until he got closer. Then he realized that all the animals were aged, sick, and dying. Some of them lay so still in the falling snow that they looked like statues.

It was a Death Caravan.

When the giant mammals of Dinotopia knew they were going to die, they made the pilgrimage to Sabertooth Mountain. There they would donate their flesh for the renewal of life. A few younger, healthy mammals, including one human, helped them make the journey, but the healthy ones did not venture into the ancestral home of the sabertooth cats.

The big cats were loners and predators who had taken an Oath of Peace not to hunt for food. Still, the Death Caravans were the only ones who visited Sabertooth Mountain.

The human waved to Moraine and Bigtusk as they approached, and many animals made welcoming sounds. Bigtusk dropped to his knees, and Moraine leaped off to greet the caravan.

Cai slapped Fatpelt's hide impatiently. After calmly munching a few evergreens, she dropped to her knees and let Cai off safely.

His legs were wobbly, but it felt good to walk. He circled the animals.

"Breathe deep, seek peace," he told them. A few of the animals grunted in reply, but most were too sick or weak to pay much attention to him. He wondered why they were stopped in Daylight Pass, with the weather getting worse.

Cai walked back to where Moraine and Bigtusk stood with the human caravan attendant, who was speaking. "We'd like to keep moving," she explained, "but we're worried about finding the trail blocked. If there really has been an avalanche—"

"Avalanche?" Cai interrupted.

Moraine frowned at him. "They heard from travelers that there has been an avalanche at Claw Pass. They don't want to continue if they can't get through to Sabertooth Mountain."

The caravan woman motioned to the gathering of giant mammals. "Some of our friends don't have much strength left. They have to save their energy to reach the sacred place."

Moraine studied Bison Trail to the east. The snow had begun to fall more heavily, and the path into the Forbidden Mountains looked dark and dangerous.

"It's several days' journey to Claw Pass by foot," said Moraine, squinting at the mountains. "There's a sky galley waiting for us in Sky City. If there's been an avalanche, I could find out quickly by flying over the mountain. Then I could come here and let you know."

The caravan woman bowed. "As you wish. We honor the wisdom and bravery of the Habitat Partners. May the snow in your path be shallow."

The big mammals standing with her echoed the good wishes in a chorus of quiet snorts and snuffles.

Moraine looked at Cai. "Rest time is over, Little Brother."

"I thought so," said Cai. "Now we'll be in a bigger hurry than before, right?"

"Right."

They said their good-byes. Bigtusk bent down so Moraine could leap onto his back. Fatpelt finished chewing and swallowing a bush before kneeling to let Cai on board. The two humans and mammoths continued south.

Cai glanced over his shoulder. Through the thickening snow he could just make out the silhouettes of the giant mammals. As he watched, the shapes dissolved into the blanketing whiteness.

They walked slowly, in silence, as the light faded completely from the sky. Even with Moraine driving them, they might not reach Sky City before nightfall. Cai pretended that he didn't care, but he did think of the warm bed he had given up at the Tentpole of the Sky and regretted his hasty desertion yet again.

Then Fatpelt stopped so abruptly that Cai nearly fell off. She snorted with alarm.

Moraine turned to look at Cai. "Now what?"

"Ask Fatpelt," he answered. "She's the one who decided to stop this time."

Bigtusk trumpeted and stamped his feet. Moraine looked up at the steep walls of rock all around them.

Cai hung on as Fatpelt whirled to stand back to back with Bigtusk. The mammoths lifted their tusks in a fighting stance.

"Come out!" shouted Moraine. "We are the Habitat Partners of these mountains. We come in peace. You have no reason to hide from us!"

They heard a low growl. A huge black shape crawled out of the shadows and stood on a ledge just over their heads. Cai gulped. It was a dire wolf—a giant carnivore with massive jaws that could crush bones.

The wolf bared his teeth and growled louder. The black and silver fur bristled on the back of his neck. Cai could see saliva dripping from his teeth.

"Can we run for it?" asked Cai quietly.

"He won't attack," said Moraine, but her voice shook a little.

More wolves slunk out of the shadows and took up positions on the ledges all around them. They growled and snapped their great jaws hungrily.

Cai wished that he was back at the Tentpole of the Sky, studying math, history, anything! It was all his fault that they were here. He gripped the ropelike knots of Fatpelt's fur tightly. No matter what happened, he had better not fall off!

Bigtusk blared a frightful sound through his trunk. Cai ducked behind Fatpelt's big ears, hoping they would give him some protection in an attack.

The wolves snarled and crept closer.

CHAPTER 2

Bigtusk trumpeted again and the air vibrated with the sound. The dire wolves howled back.

Cai slowly looked up from behind Fatpelt's left ear, expecting to see the wolves leap from the ledges. But they just held their position and snarled.

"What's going on?" asked Cai.

"Shhh!" said Moraine. "Bigtusk is talking to the wolves."

The discussion went on, with Bigtusk snorting and rumbling and the wolves snarling and growling back. Finally the big mammoth lifted his trunk to Moraine's ear and made sniffing noises. Moraine nodded several times.

"They know about the Death Caravan," she said. "They want our permission to eat the animals who die while they are stopped at the pass."

"But they're headed to Sabertooth Mountain," said Cai.

"Not according to these wolves. They say the story about the avalanche is true. In which case, this is very serious. If the caravan can't get to Sabertooth Mountain, the sabertooths will starve—or come looking for other food. It's got the wolves worried, too."

The leader of the dire wolves growled impatiently, wanting an answer.

Moraine's voice carried over the snarling of the wolves. She illustrated her words with hand motions: "I cannot promise anything. Tomorrow, I will pass over in a sky galley. I will see if there has been an avalanche. If the Death Caravan cannot reach Sabertooth Mountain, then their death will renew your life. Please wait just one more day."

The wolves howled in agreement. Cai didn't question the fact that life had to end to renew life. A tree might die to feed a sloth, and a sloth might die to feed a sabertooth. That was the way of life.

The wolves stopped howling. With ominous growls, they sank back into the caves and crannies along Mammoth Trail. A moment later, there was nothing but silence.

Moraine looked more serious than usual. "We really must reach Sky City tonight, despite the darkness." She scratched the back of Bigtusk's head. "Go slow and steady, my friend."

The mammoth nodded. He grumbled something to Fatpelt, and the mammoths walked purposefully into the snowy night.

The first sign that they were getting near Sky City was

the electric lampposts. As they got closer, they heard joyous laughter and saw children sledding on giant elk antlers.

As the mammoths climbed uphill, Cai craned his neck and spotted more sled and toboggan trails. Sky City was set inside a glacial bowl with jagged peaks all around it. A person could catch a sled on the outskirts of town and ride all the way to his destination, either in or out of the city. Two sledders came bouncing over a rise on the hill. Bigtusk had to hurry out of the way. The children continued spinning down the trail, laughing and yelling.

Cai looked after the sledders longingly. He'd much rather take a sled, or even walk, from here, but he didn't want to hurt Fatpelt's feelings. Then he remembered her playful teasing and decided that she'd understand. He bent down and whispered in her giant ear, "Can I get down now?"

The mammoth snorted in response before bending down regally to let Cai off as if he were a king. Cai groaned and staggered to his feet, thinking how good it felt to be standing. He turned back to Fatpelt. He never could have gotten this far if it hadn't been for the good-natured mammoth with the bumpy gait.

"I'll never forget your kindness," Cai said sincerely. "Thank you, Fatpelt!"

Moraine looked back at him. "Will you stop fooling around, Cai?"

"I'm taking a sled into town," said Cai. "I've been

12

here before—I know how to get around. Where do you want to meet?"

Moraine frowned. "I'm not sure that's such a good idea. I don't want anything to happen to you."

Cai crossed his arms. "Come on. I'm not going to run away. I know I've got to go to Sauropolis and see Mom and Dad."

Moraine looked at Bigtusk, who snorted. "All right," she said, "meet us at the clock tower, where the galleys tie up."

"I'll be there. I promise!" Cai stood at the side of the trail and watched Moraine, Bigtusk, and Fatpelt walk away. It was the first time he'd been alone in months, not counting those chilly nights at the Tentpole of the Sky.

As he continued uphill, Cai thought about how he had messed up his life. Here he was taking up Moraine and Bigtusk's time when they had so many important things to do. He was still surprised that they'd come at all.

At the top of a rise Sky City came into view. It was nestled in a perfect circle of snow like a twinkling ornament on a white cake. All the buildings had the smoothed, rounded look of the original igloos that were built here.

The clock tower, which was actually made up of four towers, rose in the center of town. Cai saw a sky galley floating above the rightmost tower. Of the four white towers only the middle two held clocks, both copies of the Spiral Clock in Waterfall City. Fanning out from the city like the rays of the sun were roads and sled trails brightly lit by colored lights. On the far slope, windmills spun like a squadron of phantom propellers. The wind was a constant force here, and windmills provided low-cost heat and light to the community.

With a shiver, Cai hurried down the hill, wondering where he could get a sled. He soon got his answer. Under a copse of alder trees beside a lantern was a man with a wagon full of toboggans. The man's partner, a hulking moropus, snorted as Cai walked up.

"Are you the youngster going to catch a sky galley?" asked the toboggan man.

"Yes, sir," answered Cai.

"The Habitat Partners told me you would be along. I have toboggans here for the toboggan trails. They're slower but more comfortable than the sled trails. How's that sound?"

"Great," said Cai. "Which trail should I take?"

The man pointed over a ridge. Tiny lights stretched the entire length of each trail; each trail had a different color. Blue, red, green, yellow—it looked like a stream of fireworks shooting outward from the center of town.

"You want the blue toboggan trail," said the man. "It's that one right down there, going north. If you get to intersections where there are branches, just stay in the middle. Do you know how to steer a toboggan?"

"Sure do," said Cai. "I'm not a flatlander—I'm from Thermala. Just pull on the ropes to steer, right?"

"It's an easy trail," said the man, "so just shifting your weight should be enough. Do you want to lie down or sit?"

Cai had had enough sitting. "I'll lie on my stomach, thanks."

The man pulled a toboggan off his wagon and handed it to the lad. "Take this one—it's got a soft cushion. Travel safely."

"Thanks." Cai tipped his cap to the man and hoisted the toboggan over his head. For such a long sled, it was surprisingly light. Cai knew the trip was routine for the humans who lived in Sky City, but his heart pounded with excitement nonetheless.

Cai stepped carefully down the groomed pathway of snow to the shining blue lights that ran the length of a gleaming snow chute. By the looks of the well-kept track, steering would be almost automatic. He would just have to stay calm and keep his eyes open for the unexpected.

Cai checked the curved hood of the toboggan as well as the steering ropes that lifted the front corners. His feet hanging off the end of the varnished wooden plank would serve as the brakes.

He took a running start, flung the toboggan onto the track, leaped on, and grabbed the ropes. To his disappointment, the track was so well engineered that his initial thrust didn't net him much speed. Still, it felt good to be traveling fast with the wind whistling through his hair!

He cruised along at a steady pace. Along the trail there were human and musk-oxen workers adjusting and repairing sled trails. He dragged his foot to make sure that he could brake, which he discovered worked fine.

Cai was not paying much attention as he watched the blue lights whiz past beside him until he suddenly felt a bump. The first intersection was looming in front of him! He panicked and pulled the left rope while he dragged his foot. This sent him shooting off course.

Now he was in a chute with orange lights. There were buildings all around him, plus exits where the toboggan could rise to street level. From the chute, all Cai could see were the white-domed tops of the buildings. He tried not to get distracted by them as he attempted to figure out what to do to get back to the blue trail.

Another three-way branch loomed ahead of him. This time he took the chute on the right. It seemed logical that it would take him back in the general direction of the clock tower.

The turn put Cai in a chute with purple lights, above which he could see picturesque cottage roofs lining the toboggan trail. The purple track took several twists and turns before Cai had to admit that he was completely lost. The admission made him realize that the best thing to do at this point was to get off the chute and find out where he was.

He took the next exit. The toboggan bounced up-hill, quickly losing speed. It rose out of the chute and came to a stop at the curb of a street. Cai rose to his feet, picked up his toboggan, then gaped at the sights around him.

Plodding along the street were hairy creatures of every shape and description—rhinoceroses, camels, sloths, and mastodons. Humans sat on their balconies, enjoying the procession lit by the glow of streetlamps. The homes were pueblo-style, with smaller second stories added to the first stories, which made a wide balcony around the second level.

"Can I help you, son?" asked a crackling voice.

Cai whirled around to see an ancient woman, gaily dressed in a multicolored Sherpa outfit, complete with pointed hat and booties. She carried a tiny, double-sided drum. When she twisted the handle, tiny balls on strings clacked against the sides.

He shrugged. "I'm lost. And I'm late to catch a sky galley. Where am I?"

"This here is Fortune Row," said the old woman. "I'll tell your fortune for a trade. Got anything to trade?"

Cai backed away. "I don't need my fortune told. I need to know how to get to the clock tower."

"Yes," said the old woman. "But first, I must tell your fortune. Free of charge."

She reached out and pulled the mitten off his

right hand. Then she held his hand in a surprisingly firm grip. As she stared at his hand, the fortune-teller clacked the balls on her double drum.

"You have big things ahead of you," she said. "A long journey."

Cai scoffed. "Good guess, after I said I had to catch a sky galley."

The old woman smiled and raised her eyebrows. "But your destination is not what you think it is. You have a great destiny ahead of you, young man. But you must learn to trust. And what you must learn to trust is your animal side."

"My animal side?" asked Cai.

The woman nodded. "Yes. We are more connected with the nonhumans on this island than some of us choose to remember. Stop thinking and worrying so much. Go with the flow of life. Let your instincts lead you."

Cai pulled his hand away nervously. "Please, just tell me how to get to the clock tower."

The old woman sighed. She leaned wearily against a wall. "Leave your toboggan here, so someone else may use it. Follow the flow of traffic. Turn right at the first street. Walk to the square, then take another right."

"Thank you." Cai leaned the toboggan against the wall and hurried off.

"Be brave!" shouted the old woman. "And trust others."

Cai put his head down and ran. The fortune-teller is wrong, thought Cai. I'm not headed for great things—I'm headed to Sauropolis to face angry parents. And first I have to face a couple of impatient Habitat Partners. But the old woman was right about one thing—it did no good to worry.

Cai hurried along the white streets of Sky City, past the bustling shops, puppeteers, and playful children. He stopped only once to take in the sweet aroma of roasted chestnuts wafting from a street vendor's brazier. Too bad he didn't have time to eat some. He was hungry! He hoped that Moraine had gotten them food. And that she wasn't too mad at him for being late.

Cai finally reached the square, where a group of Brontotheria were tossing oxenshoes with their horns. To the right he saw the four towers in the distance—they were easily the tallest structures in Sky City.

Tethered to the farthest tower was a sky galley. The sky galley was made up of an egg-shaped balloon that kept it airborne and a basket beneath to carry people and cargo. The basket was made out of reeds with a prow the shape of a Skybax—the famed flying creatures of Dinotopia.

Cai was nervous about flying in the airship. He had flown in a sky galley only once, when he was very little, so little he hardly remembered it at all. And this time they would be flying over Sabertooth Mountain, which was hardly a safe trip.

Bigtusk was waiting in front of the entrance of the clock tower. At Cai's approach, he trumpeted loudly. A moment later, Moraine emerged from the clock tower, her hands on her hips.

"Did you take time out for sightseeing?" she asked.

"Not on purpose," said Cai. "I got lost. Could you please yell at me *after* we eat?"

Moraine's face broke into a smile. "Okay, it's a deal. The timekeeper's family is fixing us potatoes, barley, and vegetable broth. How's that sound?"

Cai rubbed his freezing hands together. "Wonderful!"

After dinner, the timekeeper took them on a tour of the spiral clocks. Each clock was thirty feet tall and filled a tower. Cai sat on a bench in front of one of the magnificent clocks. He tried to listen to the timekeeper, but all he could hear were the pebbles falling and gears whirring inside the clocks.

He fell asleep on the bench. Moraine covered him with a blanket and let him sleep where he lay.

"Good night, Little Brother," she whispered. "I wish growing up was easier for you."

CHAPTER 3

A thousand pebbles filled a bucket and tipped it over. The pebbles cascaded into a chute, causing the hour hand on the spiral clock to jump up a notch. Cai stirred on his bench, fighting to stay asleep.

"According to the clock," Moraine said softly in his ear, "this is the time for baby cave bears to be born. So this is a good time to stay away from cave bears."

Cai sat up and rubbed his eyes. He looked with confusion at Moraine kneeling beside him. Then he saw feeble sunlight through skylights at the top of the tower.

"Is it morning?" he croaked.

"Yes, it's time for us to leave," said Moraine. She stood and tossed a pile of quilted clothing into his lap. "You'll need to dress in even more layers than usual for the sky galley. It will be especially cold when we first start up. As we rise above the clouds, the sun will warm us up a bit."

"Won't it be cold in the wind?" asked Cai.

His sister pulled on her gloves. "There is no wind

when you're traveling *with* the wind. A good galley-master doesn't fight the wind, he moves up and down until he finds the currents that are going his way. You should learn from that example, Little Brother."

She headed toward the door. "I'm going to talk to Bigtusk and see where he wants to meet on the trail. Come to the last tower in three minutes."

"What about breakfast?" asked Cai meekly.

"We'll eat in the sky." Moraine marched out the door.

Cai sighed and gazed up at the huge spiral clock. Sometimes he felt like a machine himself, always being pushed or pulled, his gears grinding.

He dressed quickly in the quilted clothing. The thin layers fit well together and were very warm. Then he strolled along a quiet corridor to the last tower and climbed a spiral staircase to the very top. The walls of the tower held an array of scrolls for reading.

Cai stepped onto the narrow roof and was blasted by a cold wind. His breath swirled in front of him for a moment before it was borne away by the wind. He could feel the hairs in his nose freeze.

A ladder made of wood and rope flopped down in front of him. He looked up to see the hull of the sky galley, floating high overhead. Cai could see huge paddles and rudders for steering on the underside of the craft. But he was worried. Up close, the sky galley looked flimsy and dangerous.

A colorful character dressed in a feathered headdress leaned over the railing. "Come on, boy, climb up!"

Cai grabbed a rung of the ladder as it started to sway in the wind. A shiver went down his back, and suddenly, the notion of flying in a little basket hundreds of feet above Sabertooth Mountain seemed very stupid. But before Cai could turn and run, he heard footsteps. He looked down to see Moraine coming up the stairs, followed by two men.

"Good," said Moraine when she saw him. "We didn't have to wait for you. Go on ahead, you can be the first one aboard."

Cai started to protest, but all of the adults were looking at him. He squared his shoulders and took a deep breath. Then he grabbed the next rung and hauled himself up, imagining that he was climbing into his tree house in Thermala.

The climb seemed to take forever, but it was really only a minute before Cai reached the railing of the sky galley. The galleymaster grabbed him under his arms and hauled him aboard like a sack of potatoes. Cai tumbled into the ship. He looked up to find an amazing assortment of instruments and gadgets.

There were compasses, sextants, telescopes, foot pedals, gearboxes, tillers, and dials to control the gas in the balloon. Surrounding them were sandbags and rigging. In the bow was a crow's nest, where the galleymaster had a wide view of air and land.

The galleymaster put his hands on his waist and

roared with laughter. "You must be a flatlander for sure."

Cai jumped to his feet, staggering as the craft moved with the wind. "I'm no flatlander! I'm only going to Sauropolis because my parents are there."

"I meant no offense," said the galleymaster with a comical bow. He was a tall, thin fellow, and his headdress made him look even taller. Fringes and feathers hung from his clothes, which, put together with the headdress, made him look more like a rag merchant than a galleyman.

"Ramón, the galleymaster, at your service. If the wind goes to a place, then so do I. We have only two rules aboard the *Sentinel.* First, do what I say. And last, don't touch anything unless I give you permission. Some of these instruments are very delicate."

Cai nodded.

Ramón pointed to a lever near the main tiller. "Especially do not touch this lever. It opens the cargo hatch. Excuse me while I help our other passenger."

As the galleyman leaned over the railing, Cai looked down at the trap door in the aft part of the ship. There were bundles of thin material and rope tied to the edges of the door—parachutes. With those, thought Cai, Ramón could drop cargo a great distance.

While questions filled Cai's mind, Ramón was helping Moraine climb over the railing and into the basket. She smiled cheerfully at Cai as she moved some boxes to make herself a seat in the bow. With incredible speed Ramón began to set instruments, twist dials, and untie ropes. When everything was done to his satisfaction, he leaned over the side of the basket.

"Cast off!" he shouted.

The two men below untied the line. Ramón hit a switch that reeled it up on a spring-driven coil. The ship lurched. Cai was knocked onto his back while Moraine held her arms out for balance.

"Sorry," said the galleymaster, "I don't normally carry passengers. But folks have to take what they can get this time of year."

"Set course for Sabertooth Mountain," said Moraine.

The galleymaster gaped at her. "Sabertooth Mountain? Why do you want to go there? Sabertooths like their privacy—that's why they live way out there."

"We're looking for an avalanche in Claw Pass," answered Moraine. "I wanted to tell you last night, but I couldn't find you anywhere."

The galleymaster chuckled. "I was sledding with the children. Guess you might say I like speed and danger."

"Then you won't mind going to Sabertooth Mountain," said Moraine, her smile sweet but firm.

"It's the air currents around Sabertooth Mountain that worry me, not the cats. Those sulfur vents shoot up like geysers. If they warmed the ground a bit, I wouldn't mind. But as it is, they just play havoc with the air currents. We aren't going to make much speed with a detour to Sabertooth Mountain."

Cai looked worriedly at Moraine. She had crossed her arms and looked determined.

"It won't take long to spot an avalanche," she replied crisply. "You'll need to drop me off somewhere to meet Bigtusk, but that would be the only stop."

Moraine's eyes narrowed as she gazed into the clouds. "We have to find out about this avalanche. If the dying mammals can't get to Sabertooth Mountain, the cats will starve. Worse, they could go to other settlements looking for food—maybe even break the Oath of Peace."

"Well, we certainly don't want that," said Ramón, moving the tiller. The craft went into a silent turn. "Hey, if either one of you wants some exercise, I could use some pedaling."

"I'll do it," said Moraine.

She jumped into the center seat and started to pedal. As the paddles spun and the rudders angled, they rose through the gray clouds. Ramón dropped a bag of sand off the side and adjusted the gas mixture. The sky galley sailed even higher until they were above the clouds. Then the sun shone down on the passengers, bright and warm.

For most of the day, they drifted over snow-capped peaks, which rose above the gray clouds like islands in a sea of mist. It was a world of peace, beauty, and sunshine. Cai wished they could stay afloat forever.

In contrast, Ramón was anything but calm. He fretted over his instruments and peered uneasily into the distance.

"I don't like my barometer," he scowled. "The clouds are getting thicker, and the temperature's dropping. Could be a storm."

"How much farther to Sabertooth Mountain?" asked Moraine. Cai guessed she was thinking about the dire wolves and the Death Caravan.

Ramón pointed northeast. "You can see it from here—it has yellowish clouds, from the sulfur vents. At top speed, we might get there in an hour. If there's a storm, there's no telling when we'll get there—or *if.*"

"I'm sorry, but this is important," Moraine insisted. "It doesn't look stormy to me."

"Well, *you* don't often see the weather from up here, do you?" asked the galleymaster. "We've got to dip below the clouds to get a look at Claw Pass, which just happens to be where the storm is, plus a lot of jagged peaks."

"We'll get there." Moraine began to pedal fiercely.

Forty minutes later, Sabertooth Mountain loomed directly ahead of them. The slender mountain stuck out of the clouds like a spike, surrounded by a strange yellowish glow. Cai could hear the rumble of thunder below them.

Ramón dashed around the galley. He set the tiller,

checked his gauges, and let gas escape from vents on the balloon.

"You can stop pedaling," he told Moraine, "but be ready to start again. There *is* a storm down there, so we can only stay under the clouds for a few minutes."

Moraine rose from her seat and grabbed one of his telescopes off its mount. "I won't need very long. Claw Pass is to the west of Sabertooth Mountain."

"I'm headed there now," said the galleyman. He let more gas escape and they plunged into the swirling clouds.

Instantly, they went from seeing everything to seeing nothing. Cai held up his hand and could barely count his fingers. He had taken his gloves off when they were in the warm sunshine, and now he had to look for them.

Then came the harsh smell of sulfur from the vents, like a wagon full of rotten eggs. Thunder rumbled all around them. Flashes of lightning glimmered eerily through the clouds. Cai crouched in the center of the galley, desperate to find his gloves but afraid to move.

Ramón stared at his instruments. "We should be breaking through the clouds any second."

Moraine gripped the rigging. She leaned over the side and peered through the telescope. "I see the ground!"

Cai rose nervously and tried to look over the side of the ship. He thought it would be a relief to break through the clouds, but when he saw the jagged peaks covered in thick snow, he changed his mind. If they crashed in *this* wilderness, no one would ever find them—not even their bones.

Moraine pointed down. "Look, there's a pride of sabertooths!"

The boy peered carefully over the railing. Far below, he could see a dozen huge cats loping through the deep snow. They seemed to be racing with the sky galley. It made him nervous to know that the meat eaters had spotted them. The cats looked far away, but one mistake by the galleyman could very quickly bring them a lot closer.

There was a loud crash of thunder before sleeting rain began to pelt them. Moraine kept the telescope to her eye, looking for Claw Pass. Ramón was busy watching his instruments and working the tiller.

The sabertooths ran under the sky galley and out of sight. Cai climbed higher in the rigging, trying to see them.

"Blast it!" shouted Moraine. "The avalanche is worse than I thought. The whole pass is covered!"

Suddenly, a spume of sulfur and steam shot a hundred feet into the air! The sky galley bounced on the hot air currents caused by the vent. Cai's feet slipped off the rigging. With a surprised yelp, he swung out of the basket.

"Help!" he shouted. He tried to grip the ropes but his fingers were too cold and numb.

"Hang on!" yelled the galleyman. He and Moraine both lunged for Cai.

But they were a second too late! Cai lost his grip. With an icy scream, he fell down, down—toward Sabertooth Mountain.

CHAPTER 4

Cai felt the wind rushing as he plunged toward the snow with a scream. He could hear Moraine and Ramón yelling, but all he could think about was that he'd messed up again. This time he was going to die and make his family even more disappointed with him!

Suddenly, he was falling through icy snow instead of sky. His fall slowed until he stopped, snow packed beneath him. He just lay there for a moment, trying to take in the fact that he was still alive. Finally, he tried to move—but he couldn't. For a second he thought that all his bones were broken. Then he realized that he was trapped in the snow!

Cai began to panic. He squirmed and wormed around until he managed to get his hand to his face. He pushed the snow away from his eyes and mouth, but that didn't help. All he could see was white. Then more snow collapsed on him and he was no better off than when he'd started. Cai tried to stay calm. He had to remember what he had learned about staying alive in an avalanche.

He heard a sound above him—a sound like digging. A rescue team! he thought. Cai tried to shout but snow fell in his mouth, muffling his words.

There came a low rumble that shook the snow around him. The digging sound began anew. Suddenly, it occurred to Cai just who his rescuers most probably were. *Sabertooths!*

Cai tried to move again, wanting to get out of the way, wanting to hide in the snow. But there was nowhere to go. He reminded himself that the sabertooths had sworn the Oath of Peace. But his mind answered that now they were starving.

As the digging got closer, the weight of snow was lightened. He felt air on his face and looked up to see a pair of tremendous claws come down. He squeezed his eyes shut. Cai felt the claws against his chest for a moment before they retracted. He opened his eyes again and stared right at a pair of canine teeth, each nine inches long.

Cai blinked and looked past the teeth to their owner, a muscular brown cat with a lighter underbelly. The sabertooth smashed his thick shoulders and neck against the snow to make room for himself. Cai struggled to get away until the big cat growled.

Cai whimpered, expecting to feel those teeth in his chest in another second. Instead, the cat lowered his head and delicately hooked Cai's belt with his teeth.

From this new angle Cai could see a red stripe of fur running down the cat's back. A moment later, he was forced to close his eyes when the beast dragged him out of the hole in the snow.

As he emerged from the snow, Cai heard the roars of the other sabertooths. He was surrounded by ferocious meat eaters!

The giant cat yanked him rudely out of the snow and tossed him down the snowdrift. Cai had no choice but to curl into a ball and roll. He thudded onto packed snow. Instantly, a dozen snarling sabertooths circled him, hissing and clawing. They were thick-necked, barrel-chested cats, built not for speed but for pouncing and delivering death blows with the daggers in their mouths.

Cai jumped to his feet and tried to run. He managed two steps before a massive cat leaped on him, pushing him into the snow. Cai rolled over onto his back and stared at his attacker. This cat was smaller and had lighter coloring than the first cat—she was probably female.

The cat inspected Cai, too. Then she leaped gracefully off his chest—something hard to do for a beast that weighed hundreds of pounds. The cat curled her canine teeth under a flange on her lower jawbone, until it looked as if she were smiling.

Cai was about to pass out from exhaustion and terror. But the terror made him jump to his feet and run again. This time a grizzled old cat with a broken tooth swiped at his legs and tripped him. Cai plowed into the snow once more, the huge cat rolling on top of him.

There was much amused growling and hissing among the cats. Slowly Cai realized that they were toying with him. They wanted to play before they killed him.

Cai changed tactics. Instead of running, he just stood his ground and stared at the sabertooths. The cats turned surly and snapped and growled at him. Suddenly, a sabertooth with dark fur bounded into the circle and took a swipe at him with his open claws. The claws tore through all his layers of clothing and raked his shoulder.

Cai cried out as pain ran down his arm. He clutched the wound and looked down at it. Blood oozed between his fingers.

"Kill me if you want to," he yelled, "but don't *torture* me!"

The dark cat turned suddenly. He unleashed his canine teeth and lunged at Cai with claws extended. Cai felt as if he were moving in slow motion as he stumbled backward. The daggerlike teeth and claws loomed over him.

At what seemed like the last moment, a flash came in from his left. In a blur, another cat hit the dark cat aside. It was the same sabertooth that had pulled Cai out of the snow! The two sabertooths rolled in the snow, biting and clawing each other in a blind fury.

The other sabertooths rooted them on with deafening roars while they fought.

As the battle continued, Cai got the impression that the dark cat was challenging the cat with the red stripe. He guessed that the red-striped one was the leader of the pride. Finally, the enraged cats backed off and crouched on their haunches, snarling at each other.

The cat with the red stripe suddenly lunged at the other one and raked his claws across his flanks. The dark-furred cat jumped into the air and scurried away. When he had gotten beyond the other sabertooths, he turned and growled over his muscular shoulder. Two or three other cats broke off from the group and loped after him.

The remaining sabertooths snapped and growled at each other. Cai held some snow to his bleeding shoulder. It stung fiercely. Cai knew there was no hope of escape, but his legs wanted to move anyway. So he started to edge away from the big carnivores.

The old cat with the broken tooth followed after him. The cat snarled and chased him back toward the others. Cai's rescuer now regarded him with a menacing look. The boy wondered if the sabertooth was deciding whether he should live or die.

"There's no meat on me," he said, plucking at his clothes. "I wouldn't even make a decent appetizer!"

Then the huge cat did something odd. He reared and twisted around, landing with his front paws planted firmly in the snow. Cai thought the cat was just playing until he did it again. This time, he planted his paws in the snow in a different pattern.

Cai stared in amazement. "The dinosaur alphabet! You *know* that?"

The sabertooth glowered at him, as if he had just been insulted. He continued to write his name in the snow. He stopped and stood back so Cai could see:

ᔕᖇᘎᘓᔕᖇᘒ

"Redstripe," said Cai. "Is that your name?"

The sabertooth bowed his head.

"It fits you," said Cai. "I just learned the alphabet myself at school. It was the *only* thing I was good at."

With his bare hand, Cai pressed the letters of his own name in the snow.

ᗩᔕ

"Cai," he said, "that's *my* name."

The way some of the other sabertooths watched him, Cai wasn't sure that he was going to live more than a few minutes. But as long as they would listen, he would keep talking to them. It was certainly better than being eaten.

Redstripe growled in an attempt to say, "Cai."

"Well," said Cai nervously, "now that we're all friends, do you think you all can help me get home?"

The sabertooths all stared at him.

"Home," Cai repeated, wondering if they understood. "Like the mountain is your home. My home is Thermala."

For a moment Cai thought there was a sadness in Redstripe's round yellow eyes. Then the sabertooth shook his head and pressed four letters into the snow.

⟵↓↓⟵↓↓↱

"Deep?" asked Cai in a puzzled voice. Then he looked around at the jagged peaks and icy terrain. They were in the heart of the Forbidden Mountains, miles away from any human settlement. The only thing deep was the snow.

Cai picked up a handful of it. The big cat growled in anger. He swiped his claw through the snow and made a deep gash. Then he pushed a mountain of snow into the middle of it.

"Oh, the avalanche," said Cai. "You must mean that Claw Pass is blocked, so I couldn't go home even if I wanted to."

He looked around at the gray clouds and the rugged peaks. Sabertooth Mountain was huge—he couldn't even see the top of it—with smaller mountains all around it. The only way in or out was Claw Pass.

Living in the mountains, Cai knew a little about avalanches. They could dump a hundred feet of snow into a gorge or pass—snow that might not thaw until late spring.

Again, he looked at the overcast sky; Moraine

must surely think he was dead. He was almost convinced of it himself. Even if Moraine knew he was alive, how could she rescue him? And hiking out on his own was hopeless for at least two more months. Could he possibly survive that long?

The sabertooths didn't seem to be starving yet, but they would be soon if they couldn't find any food. The dying animals who could fill that need were trapped on the other side of the pass.

And what would the sabertooths eat? Their Oath of Peace stated that they couldn't hunt for food. So what would they do?

Cai smiled nervously at Redstripe. He realized with a start that both of them had been wounded by the dark-furred cat. Cai touched his cut shoulder. As long as that cat was around, neither one of them would be safe.

"Who was the cat you were fighting?" he asked Redstripe. "Does he have a name?"

Redstripe nodded and wrote:

$$\text{≩⇂⋏⇧⇘→⇘⋹⇂⇂⋹}$$

"Neckbiter," said Cai grimly. "How pleasant."

Suddenly, there was a commotion nearby. Most of the big cats bounded off to investigate. As Cai looked closer, he saw they were chasing a field mouse through the snow—pouncing and batting at it. He knew exactly how the mouse felt.

Cai was left with Redstripe and two others, the female who had tackled him, and the old cat with the broken canine tooth. The female suddenly rose up and pressed her paw prints into the snow to spell out:

The older sabertooth growled grumpily, then he wrote in the snow:

Cai gulped. "Slash and Killer. I see."

He glanced over at the other cats and saw that playtime was over. One of the cats had eaten the field mouse. He supposed there were limits to the Oath of Peace. He looked back at the sabertooths whose names he now knew.

"What next?" he asked, shrugging his shoulders in a questioning way.

Redstripe yawned and glanced at Slash. She purred and glanced at the old sabertooth, Killer. Cai figured that Redstripe was the leader of the pride and Slash and Killer were his advisers. In this matter, they deferred to the elder cat, Killer.

Killer ground his teeth for several seconds. Finally, he growled, hissed, and belched. Slash cut in with a few snarls, but Redstripe growled the loudest. Like old men arguing over a checker game, the sabertooths grumbled at each other for several minutes.

Cai discovered that he could kind of figure out what the giant cats were saying. He knew that Killer had given them an answer that Slash disagreed with. But Redstripe had overruled them both. Cai just hoped they weren't debating whether to eat him for lunch or dinner.

Redstripe wrote another word in the snow:

The boy stared at them. "A council? What council? When?"

Redstripe growled and nodded around at the sabertooths. Then he drew a crescent moon in the snow.

Cai nodded in understanding. A council of sabertooths was meeting that night. He was to appear before them. He didn't want to think about what might happen to him afterward.

Suddenly, Cai felt dizzy, as if all the blood had drained from his head. With a heavy sigh, he closed his eyes and collapsed in the snow.

CHAPTER 5

Cai woke up with a strange smell in his nose: a ripe mixture of animal scents. He rubbed his eyes, but it was too dark to see. It felt as if he were in a very uncomfortable bed with a fur cover at his feet.

Cai didn't much care for fur, so he tried to kick it off the end of the bed. But the fur pushed back with sinewy muscles. Then it rumbled under its breath. Cai backed away from the weird cover. He looked around the near darkness, trying to figure out where he was.

Finally, he decided he must be dreaming in his bunk at the Tentpole of the Sky. He swung his legs off the hard bed, but the floor crunched noisily under his feet and seemed to shift. Cai jerked his legs back quickly and looked around again. Where was he?

He looked up. There was a little bit of dim light filtering through a hole in the ceiling. It wasn't bright enough to be sunlight—it had to be moonlight. There was sleepy movement all around him, but he suddenly realized they couldn't be other students from the Tentpole of the Sky. Not unless those students had taken to walking on all fours.

Then he felt a sharp pain in his shoulder. He reached up to find a large rip in his clothes. Through the rip, he touched crusted blood mixed with something sticky, kind of like tree sap. He barely remembered cutting his shoulder, or putting medicine on it.

A hulking figure sauntered toward him. Cai's memory came back in full: Sabertooth Mountain, deep snow, Redstripe, Slash, Killer, and Neckbiter. Most of all, he remembered his terror.

Now he was in their den, lying next to one of them on a stone shelf. Another sabertooth was walking toward him. What he had stepped on earlier were bones, which covered the cave floor—probably leftovers from recent meals.

Cai had just opened his mouth to scream when something soft and furry flopped into his lap. He reached down and felt a little sabertooth cub. Cai patted it until it started to gnaw on his sleeve with its sharp teeth. Then he gently set the cub aside—he didn't want any parents to get angry with him.

Cai tried to remember what the old fortune-teller in Sky City had told him. What was it? *Trust others. Use your instincts.* Right now, his instincts told him to run—should he listen to them? Or should he listen to his mind, telling him to breathe deep and seek peace?

While Cai was pondering this, a big cat padded up to him and growled in a familiar tone. It was Redstripe. He nudged the boy in the back, as if pushing him somewhere.

Cai stood up and began to shuffle forward. He put his hand on Redstripe's back so he could follow him through the darkness. Under the fur on the cat's back were knots of thick muscle. The cat made a rumbling growl as they walked along. Cai almost took his hand away, until he realized it was a purr.

Redstripe stopped suddenly. Cai felt around himself. Overhead a low-hanging stalactite was in his way. He ducked and said, "Thanks."

They walked down a winding labyrinth of pitch-black caves. Cai didn't mind the walk, as it got warmer with each step they took. Gradually, he saw a dim light far down the passage. It wasn't possible to have light this deep in a cavern, said Cai's logical mind. Then he remembered that he was walking beside a sabertooth cat.

As the fortune-teller had said, it was time to throw out logic and start living by instinct.

Instinct, instinct, Cai repeated in his head as they kept walking. Finally, they reached the mysterious light. It was a glowing globe on the end of a pole that looked as if it grew out of the rock. The globe gave off a candle's worth of light, but more globes hung ahead in a long line of glowing posts. With a light every twenty feet or so, passage through this part of the cave was much safer.

Cai looked again at the glowing ball. It was a

chunk of quartz. He knew all about luminescent minerals, but how had the sabertooth cats driven posts into the walls? And why? The outer cave, where they lived, hadn't had any lights.

Redstripe growled impatiently. Cai could see well enough to take his hand off the sabertooth's back, but he left it there as they continued down the passage.

Cai gripped Redstripe's fur when he heard a chorus of tremendous roars. The roars echoed as if the sabertooths were everywhere.

The passage widened into a vast hall of stone, with a domed ceiling held up by giant white pillars. There were statues, reliefs, and dusty murals that showed scenes of humans, sabertooths, and other large mammals together: wrestling, playing, hunting, and raising their young.

Then Cai saw the hulking forms moving among the ruins. He gulped. There were over fifty sabertooths gathered there. They jumped restlessly from broken statues to pillars to benches. Once they settled down, they roared and growled importantly.

He had never heard of sabertooths living with humans or any other species of animals. Hundreds of years ago, they had agreed to the Oath of Peace, but they never tempted themselves too much. Only the Death Caravans saw them on a regular basis, and, of course, they never returned.

Cai took a deep breath. Other Dinotopians had once lived inside Sabertooth Mountain—the proof was all around him. He thought back to his recent studies at the Tentpole of the Sky. There was considerable evidence of a past civilization on Dinotopia, before current residents could remember.

Sharp growls brought him back to the present. Ancient Dinotopian history didn't mean much when he had a council of fifty giant cats snarling at him.

He recognized only two members of the council, Killer and Neckbiter. The others were not from Redstripe's pride. Cai looked around and saw more entrances into the great hall. The cats at this meeting place came from many different prides.

Redstripe snarled loudly. The other cats finally sat or lay down among the ruins of the hall, their tails twitching back and forth impatiently. The striped cat prowled the vast room, rumbling in his deep voice. There was nobody to translate for Cai, but he knew that Redstripe was talking about him. He stood straight before the council while Redstripe pleaded his case.

Redstripe finished with a yowl, then sat back on his haunches and bowed his head. Neckbiter stood, growled ferociously, and waved his claw at Cai in disagreement. Cai could tell that there was more to the discussion than whether they should eat a scrawny boy who fell from a sky galley. Something else— something serious—was going on here.

From the corner of his eye, he spotted an old chest filled with scrolls. He hoped to have a chance to inspect the old writings. This place was a treasure trove of artifacts, but only the sabertooths knew about it!

The sabertooths took turns growling now, adding to the argument and the noise. Finally, Killer jumped into the middle of the group and made a long scratch in the dirt with his claw. Redstripe walked up beside him and made another scratch.

They're voting, Cai thought.

Neckbiter growled, turned around, and kicked dirt on him with his powerful hind legs. Cai flinched and held up his hands. He guessed that was a "No" vote.

One by one, the sabertooths voted. A dozen of them sided with Neckbiter, a few didn't vote, and the rest made scratches in the dirt. When it was all over, Redstripe had won the vote.

But what had he won exactly? wondered Cai.

The sabertooths slowly filed out of the great hall, heading in different directions. Cai thought he was safe, but Neckbiter suddenly leaped toward him. Redstripe growled in warning, but Neckbiter didn't lunge. Instead, he wrote four letters in the dust:

ᵌ⇑⇑←

Cai gulped when he read the word "food." Neckbiter wrinkled his nose and licked his long teeth with a thick pink tongue. Redstripe growled at him again. The dark cat loped off, leaving the two of them alone in the vast chamber.

The boy was in no hurry to leave. He just looked

at Redstripe and held out his hands. Patiently, the sabertooth began to write in the dust.

Redstripe's message read: "Deep snow in Claw Pass has stopped food from coming. Worried. Cubs will starve. Neckbiter and friends want to hunt, as in old days. I want to go to Dinotopians and ask them to help us. You can do this for us."

"But Claw Pass is blocked by the avalanche," Cai said. "How can we get through?"

"Dangerous," Redstripe wrote. "Only one way."

It was Cai's turn to growl as he walked away from the big cat. He wanted to go home, but he didn't want to wade through an avalanche to do so. Plus, he was worried about being caught in the snow by Neckbiter and his hungry crew. But staying here and starving with the rest of them didn't seem like a good idea either. At least now he knew why they had kept him alive—to get help from the outside.

Like the pteranodons at the Portal to the World Beneath and the tyrannosaurs of the Rainy Basin, the sabertooths were the keepers of a sacred place. Sabertooth Mountain was a place of death and renewal. But their lonely vigil kept them apart from the rest of Dinotopia. Now they were suffering because of that solitude.

Redstripe grumbled and prodded Cai in the back with his nose. Once he got the boy moving, the cat led the way to the trunk full of ancient scrolls. With reverence, he put his paw on the golden trunk.

Cai picked up the top scroll. It didn't crumble at his touch, as he had feared. The cool, dry atmosphere of the cavern had kept the rag paper in prime condition. He unrolled the scroll and gasped.

It was written in the old language that he had studied at the Tentpole of the Sky! The studies had seemed so boring then, but now he hoped he could remember enough to read them. Cai looked over at Redstripe, who was watching him intently. The cat *knew* the value of this amazing treasure.

The boy studied a few more scrolls, deciding that the one on top was the most recent. He unrolled it carefully. It was just a short note written in a hurried scrawl. Cai sat down on a white marble bench and studied it. It took him a long time to figure out what it said and he wasn't sure of the accuracy of his translation.

"Well," he said to Redstripe, "it says something like this: 'We must leave our underground cities due to…' There's a long word that I can't read. And then it says: 'There have been long discussions. Today the sabertooths say they will not leave the mountain, as a matter of'"—Cai broke off and puzzled again at the word—"'honor,' I think. The last line says: 'We hope they will be safe and breathe deep and seek peace.'"

The last line of ink trailed off down the page like a tear. Cai looked around at the magnificent hall, thinking how frightened everyone must have been to leave this place. Yet the sabertooths had stayed. Maybe that explained some of Neckbiter's attitude toward those who lived beyond the mountains.

Cai saw now what Redstripe wanted. He wanted to reopen the bridge between the sabertooths and the rest of the island. And he wanted Cai to help him accomplish the change.

Cai shook his head in disbelief. They needed Moraine and Bigtusk for a task like this—not him, not a mere thirteen-year-old boy who couldn't even go away to school successfully. He set the scroll down and walked over to Redstripe.

"I will do what I can," he said. His voice came out in a whisper. "I just want to go home."

Redstripe flicked open a claw. He drew a circle in the dust with rays coming from it. Cai had no trouble recognizing the sun. This had to mean that they were leaving on their dangerous mission in the morning.

He wanted to ask Redstripe about the dangers, but the sabertooth flopped his massive body onto the floor and fell asleep. Cai looked around to make sure they were alone. He lay down beside Redstripe and tried to use the cat's furry back as a blanket. His claw wound still hurt, but not as much as it had before.

And that's how Cai fell asleep, in the vast underground chamber, curled up next to a sabertooth cat.

CHAPTER 6

When Cai awoke, there was a dead mouse under his nose. He bolted upright and stared at the rodent. Then he gazed around at the statues and pillars in the underground chamber. He blinked a couple times. *This can't be happening to me,* he thought. *It's too unreal.*

He looked at the mouse again and wondered how it had happened to die right under his nose. Then he realized that Redstripe wasn't around and guessed where the mouse had come from and why it was there: Redstripe had brought him breakfast.

Ugh! Cai thought. He was certainly hungry, but not *that* hungry. He looked at the mouse with disgust and hoped that he'd find pine nuts on the trail.

He remembered the sabertooths chasing the mouse the day before. It wasn't only for sport—the big cats ate them. For the first time the sabertooths' plight struck him. Even an unlimited number of field mice couldn't sustain animals as big and energetic as saber-tooths.

Cai heard a noise. He looked up to see a saber-tooth walk into the chamber. "Redstripe?" he called.

The cat didn't answer. Now Cai could tell from the cat's odor that it wasn't Redstripe. After spending all night with his nose curled up in Redstripe's fur, he knew the big cat's smell.

Cai jumped to his feet, ready to run. But where could he run in this underground maze? The saber-tooth walked cautiously toward him. Cai balled his hands into fists. He wasn't much of a fighter, but he would try to defend himself.

The cat stopped and grunted in a way that sounded like laughter. Cai finally recognized the sabertooth by her lighter color—it was Slash. She looked down at his mouse and tilted her head, as if she wondered if something was wrong with it.

"Here," Cai said, gingerly picking up the dead rodent. "I'm not hungry this morning."

He gave the mouse to Slash. She took it delicately, then gulped it down in one bite. It was like feeding a peanut to a mastodon.

Cai sat down and watched as Slash prowled across the great hall, looking suspiciously at every shadow. She was smaller than Redstripe and Neckbiter, and her color was drabber. But she had a sinewy grace about her that the larger males lacked.

Suddenly, Slash whirled in the direction of the cave. The hair bristled on the back of her thick neck. Cai heard a sound, too, and he jumped to his feet.

Two sabertooths bounded out of the darkness and raced across the vast chamber. One of them was carrying something in his mouth. Cai held his breath and moved closer to Slash. The sabertooth tensed, getting ready to spring.

Then Slash sniffed the air and relaxed. Cai did the same. He recognized the scent. It was Redstripe, and along with him came the old cat with the broken tooth, Killer.

Redstripe dropped a bundle at Cai's feet. Cai jumped back, thinking it was another dead animal. But it was a bundle of clothes, including a thick coat, gloves, and snowshoes. Cai didn't ask where they had come from. He didn't want to know.

"Thanks," said Cai. He put on the coat and gloves and threw the snowshoes over his shoulder. "So we're going to Claw Pass. I'm ready."

Redstripe led the way as they slipped out one of the tunnels. Cai followed as Killer and Slash brought up the rear. Cai guessed that they were in a different tunnel than the day before. Luckily, the quartz globes shone in this tunnel, too.

Cai wondered how long Slash and Killer would be with them. An escort of sabertooths didn't make him feel any safer, because the cats seemed nervous, too.

They were plunged into darkness as the quartz lights abruptly went out. Cai heard growls ahead of them. He reached out to catch hold of the back of Redstripe's neck. Then the musky, warm smells of the den reassured him. This was where one of the prides lived, only it wasn't Redstripe's.

Cai caught sight of a tiny light far ahead of them. It looked like sunlight. He and the three cats picked up their pace and made for the welcome outdoor air.

Suddenly, there were scattered growls from the darkness. Killer ran up beside Cai as Redstripe and Slash dropped back to protect their rear. Finally, Cai and Killer squeezed out of the cave opening.

The air outside was fresh and cold. The sky was overcast, but the glare on the snow was blinding after the darkness of the cave. It was more than Cai could handle; he had to shade his eyes until they adjusted to the light. Then he saw the old sabertooth stalking ahead, searching the vast snowdrifts and rugged outcroppings for more of his kind. Cai turned back to see where the other two sabertooths were.

At that moment Redstripe and Slash wiggled through the small cave opening. Slash hissed at Cai to keep moving and pushed him ahead. Soon the odd band was slogging along a narrow trail in the snow. The cats leaped over the high drifts, but Cai had to wade through them. He thought about putting on his snowshoes, but the snow was only deep in spots.

Cai looked around at his surroundings—rock walls, jagged buttes, and snow everywhere. The towering peak of Sabertooth Mountain stood behind him, the top of it hidden in clouds. The mountain cast a shadow over everything.

The group trudged onward until Cai thought his legs would buckle. His stomach began to growl. He remembered he hadn't eaten for a long time. Worse yet, the air was starting to smell like sulfur—that rotten-egg odor. Cai also saw spots in the snow, as if a dirty rain had fallen.

Cai heard a roar behind him at the same time that he felt the ground move beneath his feet. He turned to see Redstripe running toward him at full speed. The ground shook even harder. Cai staggered to stay on his feet. Then he heard a tremendous belch!

Cai whirled around to see a geyser of steam and molten sulfur shoot high into the air—a sulfur vent! He nearly passed out from the putrid smell as the temperature shot up several degrees. Redstripe plowed into him, hooked his coat with his great teeth, and yanked him off his feet.

As the sabertooth dragged him away, Cai covered his eyes from the shower of sulfur. Redstripe threw him into a snowdrift. They both burrowed deep into the snow to hide from the deafening, foul-smelling, acidic rain.

Finally, the earth stopped its roaring. Cai poked his head out of the drift. He could see the vent on a plateau above them—there was nothing around it but scorched rock. Redstripe and Cai dug their way out of the drift while Slash and Killer did the same a few steps away.

They all hurried past the sulfur vent before it had

a chance to blow again. The cats scampered over a patch of fallen trees and boulders. Cai scrambled after them. He was actually beginning to have fun.

The band came upon a gaping gorge. Cai looked down into the dark depths. He was certain they would have to turn back, but the cats blithely took a detour by jumping from rock to rock around the chasm. Cai followed, trying not to look down.

With all the jumping, climbing, and walking, it seemed as if they must have traveled miles. But Cai knew how slow travel could be—and how vast the distances—in the mountains. Most likely, they still had a long way to go before reaching Claw Pass, let alone a village.

They passed some evergreen trees that had edible cones and nuts.

"Whoa!" cried Cai. "I need a break!"

He foraged for food while the sabertooths looked on in disgust. He looked up and noticed their expressions.

"Yes, I *am* a plant eater," he said defensively, "although I'm really like a bear, omnivorous. The humans along the coast of Dinotopia eat a lot of fish. I just choose to eat plants, okay?"

Redstripe wandered over and sniffed at the rough leaves, seeds, and twigs Cai had scrounged off the evergreen. The big cat promptly turned up his nose and walked away.

"I wouldn't talk," said Cai. "All *you* have are

mice." He ate the brittle food, trying to chew it well. Then he washed it down with a handful of snow.

There was a noise above them. The three saber-tooths took up posts all around the boy. Cai was beginning to feel like a bag of treasure. The cats surveyed the rugged ledges and buttes all around them, but all was quiet, except the wind.

Cai rose to his feet. "Okay, let's go."

The band formed a single file, with Redstripe in the lead, followed by Cai, Slash, and Killer. The wind picked up and rearranged the snowdrifts. At one point, the snow swirled and blew so fiercely that Cai could barely see where they were going. He just put his hand on Redstripe's back and kept his feet plowing ahead. When Cai thought his muscles could go no further, he hit deep snow up to his waist.

Cai stopped and strapped on his snowshoes, which spread his weight over a large area and kept him from sinking. They also made him walk like a skinny duck, he decided as he waddled up the snowbank. But for the first time, he was able to make better speed than the sabertooths. They had to slog through snow that was up to their chests.

The wind finally died down. Cai thought he could see where the jagged peaks surrounding Sabertooth Mountain pinched into one narrow draw: Claw Pass. He could see the naked slope that the snow had fallen hundreds of feet away from. But he couldn't actually see Claw Pass itself, just a big white dam of snow.

His heart sank. For the life of him, he didn't see how they were going to get over Claw Pass until the snow melted—a couple of months at the earliest. Even if a hundred mammoths started to move the snow, it would take them more than a month to finish. Cai couldn't see how the Death Caravan was going to get through in time to help the sabertooths, even if they got all of Dinotopia to pitch in.

Cai stopped and turned back to see the cats struggling to catch up with him. Should he tell them that this was pointless, that no amount of help would open this pass? The only good thing that could come out of this dangerous journey was that Cai might make it home. That in itself was enough of a reason for him to keep his mouth shut. He picked up a handful of snow and took a bite. The crisp snow crunched like food in his mouth, but it tasted only of water.

The sabertooths huffed and puffed until they were beside him. They looked very relieved to stop. Killer flopped over in the snow to take a nap, his chest heaving from exertion.

"Listen," said Cai, "we're being unrealistic. How are we going to get over that mountain of snow? Maybe I could do it in these snowshoes, if I were crazy. But one false move and I'd be back where I started—buried in the snow."

The sabertooths just stared at him. Cai waved his arms in frustration. "Aren't you listening?" he cried. "*How* are we going to do this?"

Slash stood up to her chin in the drifts. She set her head on a pillow of snow and looked wearily at Redstripe.

The big cat yawned and had to lift his foot to write an answer: "Not far away, there is a cave that comes out on the other side. We will take the cave through, if it is safe."

"*If?*" asked Cai. He felt as if he were traveling with Moraine and Bigtusk again.

Before Redstripe could tell him more, Killer rose to his feet and roared. At once, both Redstripe and Slash were on guard. Cai staggered around in his snowshoes, trying to find the cause for alarm, but he couldn't see anything in the expanse of snow and rock all around them.

Cai heard a warning growl from Redstripe. He followed the cat's eyes to a ledge of packed snow. Neckbiter and three other sabertooths came into sight at the top of the ledge. They leaped off it and came bounding through the snow!

Cai did some quick arithmetic. If Redstripe, Killer, and Slash each intercepted one of the attackers, there would still be one left to get him. They had the numbers! If a sabertooth tackled him in the snow, Cai knew he was finished.

He looked at Redstripe. The big cat had reached

the same conclusion—they had to run! Redstripe growled orders to his comrades. Slash and Killer squared off to delay the attackers while Redstripe and Cai made their getaway.

Cai waddled as quickly as he could into the deeper snow. Redstripe struggled behind him. Cai knew he had one advantage: In the drifts, the sabertooths were slower than a human on snowshoes.

The boy glanced worriedly behind him and saw Neckbiter fall back to let the others take on Slash and Killer. Their roars echoed through the pass. Cai hoped they wouldn't cause another avalanche!

Cai kept plodding doggedly on. He looked back to see that Neckbiter and another sabertooth were on his and Redstripe's tail. The two cats looked strong and powerful as they bounded through the drifts. The snow was getting deeper and deeper. Redstripe was having a harder and harder time keeping up.

Panting, the sabertooth stopped and looked plaintively at his young companion. Cai knew what Redstripe wanted to tell him. The cat had to save his strength for the fight, and Cai had to keep on moving forward. He had to get through the pass and find help for the sabertooths.

Cai waddled higher into an immense bank of snow, the angle making it harder to walk. Once or twice he lost his balance and stuck his hand in the snow up to his elbow. If he fell all the way in, he would be finished! He could hear the ferocious fight behind him, but he didn't have time to watch.

He climbed higher and higher, until the sound of fighting stopped. He took a quick glance back. Neckbiter was plowing after him! Two more cats were in the distance, but Cai couldn't tell if they were friend or foe. He could only climb on—and pray he didn't fall off his snowshoes. Cai could hear Redstripe's roars of anger and frustration in the distance.

Finally, Cai couldn't keep his balance on the steep hill any longer. He halted and watched as Neckbiter kept clawing his way upward, like a shark through a sea of white foam. Cai crouched in the snow and braced himself to be attacked by a four-hundred-pound sabertooth cat!

CHAPTER 7

Neckbiter paused to lick his chops when he was a few feet from Cai. That was a mistake. The dark cat's full weight broke through the icy crust on the snow and he found himself mired in powder up to his chin. From his snowy trap he snarled and roared at Cai.

Cai leaped to his feet. This was his only chance! Without thinking, he quickly made a snowball. He took careful aim and hurled it at Neckbiter, catching him right in the nose. The cat roared and sank deeper into the snow.

Cai threw another snowball, which hit Neckbiter in the ear. The sabertooth hissed and howled so loudly that he sounded like a sulfur vent. As Neckbiter frantically tried to claw his way out, Cai's legs began to move on their own. Treading cautiously, he inched away from the murderous sabertooth.

Suddenly, there was another growl—a deep one. Cai whirled to see Redstripe closing the gap between them with an amazing burst of speed. In a moment, he was there. Redstripe pounced on Neckbiter's back, driving him even deeper into the drift.

For a shocking moment, Cai thought that Redstripe would kill Neckbiter with a slash of his daggerlike teeth. But the leader of the carnivores held back from his animal instincts. Instead, he just drove Neckbiter deeper into the snow. Finally, Redstripe leaped off the other cat's back and followed Cai.

Now Cai and Redstripe had to hide their trail as well as put some distance between themselves and Neckbiter, so rather than continue up the slope, they headed crosswise. Cai wanted to know what had happened to Slash and Killer, but there was no time to find out. They had to keep moving as quickly as possible.

A sudden wind came up and started rearranging the snowdrifts once more. For the first time, Cai didn't mind, as the swirling snow covered their escape more effectively than their change of direction. Behind him he could see nothing of Neckbiter or the other sabertooths. He couldn't even see where they had left Neckbiter in the snow.

Cai would have breathed a sigh of relief, but he was out of breath. He could barely make his legs work by the time he and Redstripe staggered to firm ground. They crawled behind an outcropping of rock and collapsed. Redstripe and Cai just lay there, watching gray clouds move lazily over Claw Pass.

Finally, Redstripe rolled over and looked at Cai

wearily. Cai could see cuts and streaks of blood in the sabertooth's thick fur. He suddenly felt worried about the heroic leader. If they actually made it to a village, how could Cai ever repay him? He feared they wouldn't be able to do much about the avalanche in Claw Pass.

Cai decided that what the sabertooths really needed was a voice in Dinotopia. They were so isolated that to the rest of the island dwellers they were hardly more than stories. The sabertooths needed to claim their Dinotopian heritage and have their history included in the library in Waterfall City. Their neighbors shouldn't wait until they ran out of food to notice them!

Redstripe dragged himself to his feet and sniffed the air. He rumbled under his breath. It was time to go. After twenty minutes of searching, Redstripe found a wide trail in the snow. He followed it very cautiously. Cai could see why. It wasn't a sabertooth trail, it was a *bear* trail—he could tell by the tracks. And they were recent tracks, since the last snowfall.

Cai stopped suddenly. "We aren't going into a bear's cave, are we?"

Redstripe gave him a guilty look and trotted off down the trail. Cai watched him go, wondering what he could do to change the cat's mind. Going into a bear's cave was insane! Of course, trying to cross an avalanche was insane, too, and so was just being on Sabertooth Mountain.

Cai looked behind him at the towering mountain and the snowy wilderness. It would probably be beautiful here in five months. During the height of summer, this whole area would blossom with wildflowers. But right now it was nothing but snow, rocks, and death. Above, the clouds were thickening, as if a storm was coming. Even without a storm, it would be night before too long. Bears or no bears, they would be forced to seek shelter.

Maybe they could negotiate their way around the bears, Cai told himself. After all, they were only passing through. Surely Redstripe would be able to bargain with the local bears. Wouldn't he?

They were moving away from Claw Pass and deeper into a box canyon that branched off the main draw. It occurred to Cai that Redstripe would have preferred to climb over the avalanche rather than take this route. The sabertooth was only going this way out of desperation.

Redstripe stalked ahead in a crouch, ready to spring, while Cai tried to remember everything he knew about cave bears. They slept most of the winter, but they didn't hibernate. They were solitary creatures, so you were only likely to meet one bear at a time—unless you met a mother with cubs, in which case you were in big trouble.

This is the time for baby cave bears to be born. So this is a good time to stay away from cave bears, Moraine had told him. Cai looked at the fresh tracks and got a sick feeling in his stomach. He wondered if Moraine had had some kind of premonition, for her to tell him that before they had set out. It seemed like years ago that he had climbed into the sky galley.

The tracks they were following veered to the right. Redstripe made his own path to the left. They started climbing up into the ledges and ridges that ran alongside the narrow canyon. It was tougher than before, but Cai was relieved to get away from the bear tracks.

They reached the end of the canyon and climbed upward on a small ridge. The winds had stripped the rock wall of snow, but it was still icy and treacherous. Cai was sure that he would slip and fall at any moment, but his legs kept going.

They edged along until Cai was about to yell at Redstripe that he couldn't go on. Just then he saw their destination: a small hole beneath an overhanging ledge. The opening looked hardly big enough for Cai to crawl into, let alone Redstripe or a bear. But the sabertooth kept inching toward the opening, and Cai kept on inching behind him.

By the time they reached the mouth of the cave, they were clinging to the rock like lizards. Cai was so scared of falling that he almost dove into the hole. He would have been happy to meet a bear inside the cave if it meant getting off that narrow ledge. He squirmed through the opening into a narrow passage with rows of stalactites and stalagmites. It was like being in a forest of stone trees and vines. The stalactites hung so low that he had to crawl along on his stomach.

There was a tiny bit of light coming from the hole behind him, which disappeared as soon as Redstripe filled the opening. Cai stopped to wait for the big sabertooth, but Redstripe snarled at him to keep moving. The cat was having a hard time getting through the hole, and it was making him grumpy.

After Redstripe finally squeezed through, there was light again. Cai inched forward on his stomach, feeling ahead with his hand for sudden drop-offs. Only his trust for Redstripe kept him going—that and the fact that it was getting warmer as he crawled deeper into the cave. He could hear the sabertooth behind him, breathing hard on the backs of his legs. This was fine with Cai, as he liked having the big cat near, but he wished Redstripe were in the lead instead.

It became darker and darker. Soon Cai was navigating by touch and instincts. Outside the cave, he had felt like a lizard clinging to a ledge; inside, he felt like a blind newt.

Suddenly, the passage widened and angled sharply downward. Cai cried out as he fell, but Redstripe hooked his pants leg with his canine teeth. The big cat lowered the boy about four feet down to the next level, then he slid down after him.

Cai could stand up in this part of the cave. That was both a relief and a worry, because if he could walk through here, then so could a bear. Beside him, Redstripe sniffed the cool air for enemy scents. The cat set off down the dark passageway. Cai followed, gripping the folds of Redstripe's neck.

They were headed downhill again. It got so warm that Cai took his jacket off. The air smelled like the foundry at Volcaneum, which Cai had visited with his parents. It must be his imagination, he decided. Cave bears could not be making metal goods down here. Stranger yet, he could see a flickering glow of light in the distance. It wasn't like the quartz globes—this was more like the light from a campfire.

Redstripe moved warily toward the glow, and Cai followed. Thick roots twisted along the ceiling and walls of the cave, clinging to the rock. They drew closer to the light, and the heat became like that from a blast furnace. Cai looked around and wondered if they were approaching the ruins of a foundry, even though the cave looked natural.

Near the end of the passage Redstripe fell back and looked sheepishly at Cai. Cai wasn't sure what was going on but took the lead. The passage opened out on a hot cavern. It was a different kind of underground palace, one made by the chaos of nature.

In the center of the cavern was a lake of fire. Dark tar floated on the surface, bubbling and burning. Flames roared toward the ceiling and filled the chamber with strong fumes. Amazingly enough, Cai's mind was still working. The sight of the burning tar on the water gave him an idea.

Redstripe was shrinking against the rock wall, his

eyes searching for another exit.

"It's okay!" shouted Cai. "Let me try something."

The walls in this chamber were also covered with roots. Cai broke off a long one. He was happy to find that the root was perfect for his purpose—dry, but not too dry. He took off one of his shirts and tore it into strips. Redstripe watched him curiously.

Cai tied the rags to the end of his stick. Then he walked cautiously toward the burning lake. If his crazy idea worked, it would solve two problems at once: that of light and that of protection. The sweat rolled down Cai's face as he reached across the flames and dipped the rags into the burning tar. The thick substance stuck to the rags. Cai lifted the stick. Now he had a burning torch!

Redstripe growled his approval. Though he was afraid of fire, he understood its usefulness.

Cai kept the first torch burning and prepared two more. After that, he couldn't spare any more clothes. He figured that as one torch started to burn out, he would light another one. When all three burned out, he would be back where he started.

Redstripe had spotted another passage. He skirted the fire and jogged forward, looking back to check on Cai, who was right behind him with the torches. They entered the new tunnel. With Cai carrying light, the sabertooth could run ahead and scout the passageway.

In the maze of narrow passages, Cai completely lost his sense of direction. But he had light, and the temperature was pleasant. The boy was almost feeling relaxed when Redstripe growled in warning. Cai stepped cautiously forward, wielding the torch like a weapon. The cave widened. Now he finally smelled the animal scents he had expected.

Redstripe sniffed a pile of gigantic bones scattered on the floor of the cave. They were much bigger than human bones—they had to be sloth or mammoth. They were old bones, picked clean long ago, and Cai was able to step around them without feeling queasy.

He kept telling himself that cave bears were solitary creatures, and that it would be rare to find one. Besides, if they did stumble across a bear, it would probably be asleep. Then they could hurry past quickly and quietly. Still, Cai checked his torch to make sure it was in no danger of going out.

Suddenly, without warning, a monstrous black bear lumbered into their path. Redstripe was caught off guard. All he could do was hiss and back up toward Cai. Cai waved his torch but ended up hitting Redstripe in the rump with it. The frightened cat snarled at him, and Cai jumped back, holding the torch high over his head.

The cave bear blinked sleepily at them. He was a roly-poly mass of fur, with a flat face that was almost comical. It was a shock when he finally roared. Then the cave shook so hard that chunks of dirt clattered down upon their heads. With a bellow, the bear charged, galloping on all fours and sending bones flying in all directions. Cai and Redstripe stumbled over each other to get away, but the bear was on them in seconds.

Cai had no choice but to whirl around with the torch and shove it in the bear's nose. The bear howled and reared up on his hind legs. He was so tall—almost ten feet—that he hit his head on the roof of the cave. He groaned and flopped to the ground.

Cai and Redstripe fled.

CHAPTER 8

Cai's torch was flickering, so he had to slow down to keep it from going out. He stole a glance behind him. The cave bear was nowhere to be seen.

"Wait!" he called to Redstripe, panting for breath. "The bear's not coming after us. He hit his head. Maybe we should go back and make sure he's okay."

Cai didn't know why he should be so worried about a cave bear. But they had trespassed in his cave, surprised him out of a deep sleep, stuck fire in his face, and made him hit his head. Cai felt responsible. He really did want to know that the bear was all right, even if it was dangerous.

"Now I am definitely crazy," he muttered to himself.

Holding the torch in front of him, he headed slowly back down the passage. Redstripe growled at him, but when the cat saw it wasn't going to do any good, he followed at a safe distance.

Cai found the bear sitting in the middle of the cave, gingerly touching his sore nose and head. When he saw the intruders, he huffed, snorted, and backed away from them. Cai realized that the bear was afraid, so he put the torch behind his back.

"It's okay, we won't hurt you," he said in a soothing voice. "We're only passing through."

The bear studied them curiously. It was certain that he had never before seen a sabertooth and a human traveling together in a bear cave. He shook his great furry head as if he were seeing things.

Redstripe stayed behind Cai. He probably didn't want to frighten the already scared animal. Cai decided to take a chance on the bear also knowing the dinosaur footprint language. He knelt down and used his hand to write a single word in the dust:

子山山个山

"Peace," he said to the bear, pointing at his writing.

The bear stared at the markings in the dust and wrinkled his flat nose. Cai decided to try a different approach. He had lived with big mammals all his life in these mountains, and he knew a few sounds that had meaning to giant sloths. Bears were very vocal. Cai guessed that they might have a similar language.

As the bear and the sabertooth looked on, Cai knelt down. He pawed the ground and made mewling sounds. This was to show that they were in a lesser position and were seeking help from the mighty bear. Redstripe looked a little shocked. Cai turned to him and glared. The big cat bent down in a subservient position with a sigh.

After their display of submission, the bear puffed his chest out and growled importantly. Cai grinned, knowing he had made his point. If only they could get this bear to escort them through the cave. Maybe the bear could also smooth things over with any other bears they might meet.

Cai drew a big mountain in the dirt, surrounded by several smaller mountains. Then he added a jagged line that was supposed to be Claw Pass, plus some more lines through the line to show the avalanche. Cai looked up. The bear was studying the map intently. Cai took hope and drew a wiggly line that went through the mountains and around the pass. Then he sat back on his heels and pointed to the caverns around them.

The bear snorted once, leaned over, then held a huge forepaw over the map. Cai feared that he was going to wipe it out. Instead, the bear added little circles with a giant claw that Cai took to represent cave openings. When he was done, the bear grunted with satisfaction.

Cai pointed to himself and Redstripe, then he pointed to the part of the map that showed a cave opening beyond Claw Pass. It couldn't be any clearer. The bear gazed warily from the boy to the sabertooth. Cai could see that Redstripe was the bear's primary worry, so he reached over and patted the big cat on the head to show that he was friendly. Redstripe gave him a disgusted look, but overall took the patting fairly well.

With a grunt, the bear lifted his bulk onto his stocky legs and ambled off. Cai and Redstripe followed. As they walked, the sabertooth looked around nervously. Cai held his torch low, so as not to spook any more sleeping bears. For the first time, he was beginning to feel as if they might pull off a miracle and make it through Claw Pass alive.

Then his logical mind squashed the hope—because after they left sabertooth territory, there was still a long way to go. And when they got to a village, Cai would have to be a diplomat, which he wasn't looking forward to at all. It was a job for Moraine—somebody older and more experienced and more, well, diplomatic.

Besides, Cai didn't know what anyone could even do about the avalanche! It was the sun's job to take care of snow, and it would do so in its own sweet time. He looked at Redstripe, knowing that the sabertooth was shouldering a lot of responsibility, beginning with the welfare of his pride. Until Claw Pass was open, the sabertooths would go hungry.

Or maybe they would go hunting.

Suddenly, Redstripe stopped. He whirled around and snarled. He was at the rear of the party, growling at a part of the cave they had just passed through. Ahead, their guide bear stopped, too. The bear's lips

curled back from his jagged teeth and he roared ferociously—only he was roaring at Redstripe in warning.

"Wait a minute," said Cai, trying to sound calm.
"What is it, Redstripe? What do you see?"

The sabertooth peered into the darkness behind
them, then he shook his head and lay quietly on his
stomach. The bear grumbled under his breath, but he
was satisfied with the cat's submissive attitude. He
turned around and continued on through the tunnel.

Cai whispered to Redstripe, "Apparently, he's the
only one who's allowed to growl down here."

The cat hissed unhappily and glanced back over
his massive shoulder. Something was bothering him,
but there was no time to find out what, as their guide
was plowing ahead through the caves.

A few minutes later, Cai's first torch started to
sputter. He halted a moment to light another one.
The bear stopped and watched impatiently, as if he
didn't have time to wait on people who needed fire to
walk through a cave.

"Sorry," said Cai.

The bear grunted and headed off again. Then
trouble arrived from ahead as another bear came roaring out of a side chamber! The attacker tossed their
guide against the wall. He fought back with all his
strength, but he wasn't a match for the enraged bear.
Cai could see a small lump of fur crouching in the
mouth of the side cave—a bear cub!

Redstripe jumped into the fray, growling. He took

a swipe at the mother bear. In her protective fury, she kept beating up the other bear, ignoring the cat and the boy. Finally, Cai had no choice but to lunge at the mother bear with his burning torch.

That got her attention, and she went berserk! Fire or no fire, she chased Cai down the length of the cave, until he whirled around and raised the torch in front of him. But nothing would stop her!

Just when Cai thought he was finished, a ferocious roar caught the mother bear's attention. She turned to see Redstripe in the mouth of the small cave, stalking the bear cub. Cai knew it was a desperate attempt to distract the female, and it worked. The mother bear roared and charged after the sabertooth.

Cai dropped his torch in the confusion. When he bent down, another dark shape ran past him. It was neither Redstripe nor their guide, because Cai could see both of them. He forgot about it a moment later when he picked the torch up again. The scene in front of him was pure chaos.

Redstripe was darting away from the female bear. Finally, Mom began to see that it might be better to stay close to her baby. She planted herself in the entrance of her chamber and snapped at the travelers as they made their escape, her teeth missing them by inches.

After that their guide bear didn't act so important anymore. Cai nearly laughed when it occurred to him that this was a good time of year for even *bears* to avoid mother bears.

Then he remembered the animal that had rushed past him. He wanted to ask Redstripe if he had seen it, but there was no time to stop and wait for Redstripe to write an answer out. Redstripe looked irritable, anyway, glancing around the cave and shaking his head.

In the distance, another patch of light came into view. It looked like a sliver of sunlight. Cai and Redstripe sped up until they were right behind the cave bear. He scuffled along a bit faster, too, and his tongue lolled out of his mouth.

The bear was the first to reach the slit in the wall where two enormous boulders had collided centuries before. Cai felt a sudden chill. High overhead was a slice of sky.

The bear squeezed through the opening. Cai and Redstripe followed eagerly into a deep hollow with boulders all around. The boulders curved overhead into a partial roof that sparkled with packed snow. But on the ground was an even more stunning sight—massive bones covered every inch. There were giant rib cages a man could stand inside and huge ivory tusks. Everything was layered with frost and icicles, which glittered in the fading sunlight. The bones looked as if they were made of crystal.

This was the center of Claw Pass, the sacred place

where the great mammals came to die. Snowdrifts surrounded them, held back by a mass of boulders and bones. It was a bleak scene of death and beauty—white bone against white snow.

Cai watched the sabertooth and the cave bear as they quietly gulped snow. He set his torch down near the mouth of the cave, then he grabbed a handful of snow for himself. It was great to be outdoors again after suffering through the tight, smelly caves. Unfortunately, they were snowed in and couldn't go anywhere from here except back into the caves.

The bear scrounged for food among the bones, but he didn't find much. He would soon figure out that the Death Caravans were not getting through to Claw Pass, but he had other options. He could eat plants, or he could just go back to sleep and wake up later, in the spring. He had plenty of fat to live off until winter ended.

Redstripe sat and looked solemnly at the great bones. This was a holy place for him, too. It represented the bond between the meat eaters and the plant eaters, who gave their bodies to renew the lives of others. Without that bond, the sabertooths could not exist.

The boy sat down beside the big cat and told him about the other animal that he'd seen in the bear's cave during their meeting with the mother bear.

The sabertooth looked at Cai with his intense yellow eyes and nodded. Yes, Redstripe had seen it, too.

"What was it?" asked Cai.

Redstripe opened his mouth to show off his enormous teeth. He was telling Cai that it was another sabertooth who had run past them in the melee with the mother bear.

Cai sat in the snow, dumbfounded. It *had* to be Neckbiter, or one of his followers. If it were Slash or Killer, they would have stopped to help. What was Neckbiter doing? Where was he going? And why? Cai looked at his companion and realized why he was so grumpy. Not only had they been followed, they had been passed.

Cai could see that Redstripe wanted to move on. But the bear wanted to forage, and Redstripe waited patiently but tensely. A short time later, it was getting dark and cold. Now the bear was ready to move on. He lumbered to the slit in the rocks and somehow squeezed through. Redstripe followed him, with Cai bringing up the rear.

He grabbed his torch, and before going back into the cave, he looked back one last time at the graveyard of giant mammals.

If Cai had looked up at that moment, he would have seen a sky galley cruise over Claw Pass. Moraine was peering over the side of the galley, her long black hair trailing in the wind. She focused a powerful telescope on the ridges of snow, but she couldn't see any tracks.

She tried to be hopeful. Maybe the wind had

blown over the tracks, or maybe it was just too dark.

Or maybe Cai was dead.

Moraine leaned back into the airship. The galley-master, whose gray hair flowed from under her fanciful headdress, clicked her tongue sadly.

"It's getting dark, Missy," said Keshan, the galley-master. "We've got to be going."

Moraine pointed anxiously at the ground behind them. "But I know I saw snowshoe tracks back there! No animal makes tracks that look like that."

"Have you seen some of these cave bears?" asked Keshan. "They have pretty big feet. But if the boy had snowshoes, he might be able to get over the pass. Did he have snowshoes?"

Moraine's shoulders slumped. "No. He didn't have any equipment at all."

"And you still think he's alive?" asked Keshan doubtfully. "Missy, you know these mountains better than that."

Moraine sat dejectedly in the bottom of the sky galley. "Yes, I know the chances of him being alive are slim. But I have to try to find him."

Moraine hit her fist on her knee. "It was *my* fault! I shouldn't have brought Cai with me on such a dangerous journey! But I was in a hurry—I thought I could do two jobs at once. No one was even watching him when he climbed up those ropes. I should have sent him to our parents and waited for another sky galley."

"You're being too hard on yourself," said Keshan. "Maybe you learned a lesson. None of us are too old for lessons. The important part is, you're doing all you can to find the boy and help the sabertooths."

Moraine looked up with weary eyes. "Can we trust Ramón? He's got a very important assignment."

"Don't worry. Ramón won't let you down."

"Good," said Moraine. "We can't let the saber-tooths starve. They don't exist anywhere else on earth."

"I know." The galleymaster adjusted the gases in the balloon and tossed a sandbag over the side. They began to rise slowly out of Claw Pass. "Where now?"

"Sulfur Springs," said Moraine. "It's the closest village, so I told Bigtusk to meet me there. We'll continue our search for Cai. I'll also keep a watch on things around here until Ramón gets back."

Keshan glanced over the side of the galley. "I don't think anyone is going to get through that pass. It's too blocked up."

"I guess you're right." Moraine looked up as thick clouds engulfed the sky galley. She felt as if the dark winter would never end.

Cai had no idea what time it was when they finally emerged from the mountain again. All he knew was that it felt great to step outside and see the sky. Through a hole in the clouds he could even see a sprinkling of stars. Not only that, but the giant snowbank was behind them. They had made it through Claw Pass!

"Yippee!" he shouted.

The bear turned and growled at him, but Cai could only smile. Their guide had done them a great favor, and had made the impossible a little less so. Cai's last torch was still burning. He plunged the stick into the snow to put out the flame. Then he walked over and handed the torch to the startled bear.

The huge animal looked curiously at the unlit torch and touched it with his paw. It was clear that he considered the burnt root to be a fine reward. The cave bear bowed his head and made a series of grunts. Cai did the same in return.

With a glance at Redstripe, the bear picked up his prize in his teeth and lumbered back into his lair.

The sabertooth grumbled wearily and flopped down on the snowy ground near the mouth of the cave. Cai saw tracks in the snow, and he thought about Neckbiter. Where was the rogue cat? At least they had a clear view for miles around, so Neckbiter couldn't sneak up on them.

Cai lay down next to the sabertooth, leaning his head on the cat's warm, furry shoulder. In a few seconds, they were both asleep.

CHAPTER 9

A golden streak of light slid across the snow toward Claw Pass as the sun peeked between two mountains to the west. The sunlight flowed over Cai and Redstripe, and they stirred with the sudden warmth.

The boy blinked up at the dawn, but he couldn't bring himself to wake. Instead, he snuggled deeper into Redstripe's thick fur. The cat was beginning to smell much better, thought Cai, drifting back into a pleasant sleep.

Redstripe had other ideas, however. He rolled over and stood up. Cai's face dropped into the snow.

"Hey!" growled the boy, sitting up. "What's wrong with getting a little more sleep? We walked all day and half the night to get here."

The cat looked at him and yawned. His giant canine teeth pointed outward like spear tips. Cai marveled at how wide the cat was able to open his mouth.

Cai swallowed a mouthful of snow to quench his thirst. He took his first look around the rugged canyon on the other side of Claw Pass but couldn't see anything to eat, only a few leafless, stunted bushes poking out of the snow. Then he saw sabertooth footprints in the snow. Redstripe saw them, too. Neckbiter had come this way.

Cai didn't know this part of the Forbidden Mountains, or where the closest village was. But he knew there was still a long way to go. They could follow Neckbiter's footprints, but they didn't know where he was headed. Cai tried not to think about what a hungry, discontented sabertooth might do in one of the villages.

Then Cai remembered that he, Moraine, and the mammoths had stood at the crossroads of Mammoth Trail and Bison Trail. That was where they had met the Death Caravan. Bison Trail might not be the *closest* route to a village, but it should get them there.

"I think we should try Bison Trail," said Cai. "Do you know where it is from here?"

Redstripe gave a low growl and nodded in the direction of Neckbiter's tracks. The great cat padded off, while Cai pulled his coat tighter around his thin body. He wished he had those shirts he had used for torches. Against all logic, he felt sad about leaving and wondered if he would ever return to Sabertooth Mountain.

Cai ran to catch up with Redstripe. They walked in silence for an hour. Then big, puffy snowflakes started to fall, and soon Neckbiter's tracks were completely covered. The companions walked on through the snow, although Cai wondered if they were on the Bison Trail, or just wandering.

Then they found something that took the guess-work out of it—a dead bison in the snow, half eaten. Cai didn't want to look too closely at the body, but a quick glance told him that the bison had been quite old. Cai figured that he had probably been trying to get to Sabertooth Mountain when he ran up against the avalanche.

Redstripe had no problem with eating leftovers, so Cai wandered away to leave the big cat to the first real meal he'd had in a long time. Cai looked out at the rugged buttes and ridges of the Forbidden Mountains. Whatever animal had left the bison half eaten must have been in a hurry. It was probably Neckbiter.

Redstripe brought over a piece of the bison. Cai shook his head. Redstripe kept nudging him, but Cai just couldn't force himself to eat it. Finally, Redstripe turned away with a shrug and they set back on the trail. With food in his belly, Redstripe was much happier. Cai tried to keep up with him, but it was impossible. Finally, Redstripe circled back and crouched down in front of the boy. He nodded toward his broad, tan back.

Cai blinked in amazement. "You want me to *ride* you?"

Redstripe made a growling purr and nodded his head again. Cai was too weak to argue, so he climbed upon the cat's furry back. To his surprise, it was a fairly comfortable seat—much better than a mammoth. His feet dangled off the side, but they didn't touch the ground. As the sabertooth walked along, Cai could feel the cat's powerful muscles working.

At midday, Redstripe stopped in front of some bushes with a few remaining leaves and seedpods on them. Cai jumped off his back and gobbled up the few handfuls of food. He felt much better, but Redstripe still insisted that he ride on his back. Cai didn't protest too much because he was actually enjoying the ride. For the first time in his life, he felt truly bonded to an animal.

Living in Thermala, he knew lots of people who were best friends with dinosaurs and giant mammals. Moraine and Bigtusk were a good example, as were all the other Habitat Partners. Some people bonded to animals as young children, and they never left each other's side. Other people bonded with animals as adults, once both of them learned a trade.

But not everyone made friends with a great beast. Some dinosaurs and great mammals stayed in herds, although they often worked with humans on earthmoving projects. Likewise, some humans bonded to each other, like Cai's mother and father. They worked as a team and traveled all over Dinotopia, doing surveys for roads and buildings. When Cai and Moraine were younger, his parents used to take them everywhere. Then Moraine left to be a Habitat Partner and it was just Cai and his parents until he left for Tentpole of the Sky. But going away had made him feel left out, as if he had no place on the family team anymore.

But now he had Redstripe. Cai found himself thinking beyond just getting help for the sabertooths. Maybe he and Redstripe could start a new chapter in the story of the sabertooths. Or if nothing else happened, at least Cai had made a true friend.

As they rode along, the boy thought about Neckbiter. Was there any way to convince the sabertooth to try and let them help? Cooperation was the key on Dinotopia, but everyone needed to participate for it to work.

Suddenly, Redstripe stopped and growled. Cai felt the rough fur bristle on the back of the cat's neck.

"That's close enough!" snapped an angry voice.

Boy and cat looked up at a snowy ledge. All Cai could see was the top of a man's head and the scoop of a shovel. The man crawled out to the edge of the ledge and glared down at them.

"What is this," he grumbled, "a sabertooth parade? Twenty years I've been mining quartz up here, and I've never seen a sabertooth. Now I've seen *two* in one day! Can't they stick to their own mountain?"

Cai stroked the back of Redstripe's neck. "It's okay, he won't hurt us," he assured the cat.

The sabertooth growled as if he saw no reason to relax. After all, the man was pointing a large shovel at them.

"We're just passing through," said Cai. "We don't mean you any harm."

"Oh, sure," scoffed the man. "That other sabertooth chased me up here, and then he went after poor Jasper. He's probably chased him all the way back to the village by now. Wouldn't you say that getting eaten is *harmful*?"

"I'm traveling with a sabertooth," said Cai, "and I haven't been eaten. Neither have you, unless you're a ghost."

The man scowled. "That's only because I used my shovel. I've been up here since morning, and I'm not coming down. I'm staying put until I'm sure there are no more sabertooths on this trail."

Cai climbed down off Redstripe's back and walked slowly toward the man. "I'm Cai, and this is Redstripe. What's your name?"

"Marcus," answered the man.

"Why don't you tell us what happened?"

Marcus cleared his throat. "Well, Jasper and I were out here chipping shale and looking for quartz. Jasper's a long-necked camel. That other cat might be in trouble if Jasper gets in a good kick—he's about twenty feet tall, with long legs. Anyway, he and Jasper are probably at Sulfur Springs by now."

"Sulfur Springs?" asked Cai. "Is that village close to here?"

"Closest one," answered the man. "It's a small village, but we call it home."

Cai turned to Redstripe and whispered, "We'd better get going. Neckbiter could cause lots of problems in a village."

He turned back to the frightened miner. "Which way is it to Sulfur Springs?"

"Are you going with that sabertooth cat?" asked the man. "Does he follow the Oath of Peace?"

"Yes, he does," answered Cai. "Almost all the sabertooths follow the oath, but they're starving right now. We've got to find a way to help them. They need to eat. Please tell us which way to the village. It's important."

Marcus looked up at the falling snow. "Their tracks are probably gone, so you'll have to look for landmarks. Go down this pass until you come to Rhino Rock—it's a rock that looks like a woolly rhino's head with two horns. Go to the left, the way the horns are pointing. After a while, you'll smell the sulfur and see smoke in the distance. Just head straight for the smoke."

"Thank you," said Cai. "Do you want to come with us?"

The man looked warily at Redstripe. "No, thanks. Too many strange things going on this morning—I'm just going to sit and watch. I've got food and a tent—I can stay out here awhile."

"Suit yourself," said Cai. "Good luck."

"Good luck to you, too," said Marcus. "And if you see Jasper, tell him I'm okay."

"I will," promised Cai. He climbed up on Redstripe's back. They set off down the trail with a curtain of snow falling all around them.

"This could be a problem," Cai said. "No one is used to seeing sabertooth cats. And Neckbiter is terrifying. I want you and the sabertooths to be able to come and go as you please, not be feared."

Redstripe grumbled, as if to say he would wait to see.

They had no trouble finding Rhino Rock—it did look just like the head of a woolly rhinoceros. The Bison Trail went right, but they turned to the left and found themselves in a narrow canyon. Cai looked around nervously. For the entire journey, he kept expecting Neckbiter to jump out and attack.

The sun was starting to slide behind the mountains when they spotted smoke in the distance. The wind shifted, and they could smell the harsh odor of sulfur. The smell wasn't as bad as it was near the sulfur vents on Sabertooth Mountain, but it was bad enough. At least they were headed in the right direction.

They saw no sign of Neckbiter or the camel named Jasper. But that didn't mean much, because there were a dozen small canyons and caves they could have vanished into. Cai hoped that Neckbiter had given up the chase and gone somewhere to sleep off his earlier meal of bison. Cai himself was so tired that he could barely stay awake.

As they neared the village of Sulfur Springs, Cai could see twinkling streetlamps and tiny cottages painted in bright, cheerful colors. In the center of town was a brick building with yellow smoke curling from the top of its chimney. The building probably housed the bubbling sulfur springs that gave the town its name.

The sleepy village reminded Cai of Thermala, which had dozens of springs and mineral baths. People, mammals, and dinosaurs came from all over Dinotopia to bathe in Thermala's soothing waters. Of course, Sulfur Springs was much smaller than Thermala, but it had the same kind of warm, friendly glow. Cai felt instantly at home.

Even as he was relaxing, Cai could feel Redstripe's muscles tightening under his fur. The boy couldn't blame the big cat for being nervous. Cai was going home, but the sabertooth was braving an unknown world in which he was an unknown, too. Would he be received as an ambassador or a predator?

They passed the first row of cottages on the outskirts of town. The blue, green, and white houses were cheerful, but the streets were empty. Cai expected to see children playing, workers heading home from their labor, and camels lighting the streetlamps.

They were probably all inside eating dinner, Cai decided quickly. His own stomach growled at the thought of hot broth, fresh bread, and steaming vegetables.

They rode a little farther into town. There was still no sign of people or mammals. Cai didn't expect a welcoming party, but he didn't expect the town to be deserted either.

Where was everybody?

He could feel Redstripe's heart beating rapidly. He knew the giant cat was afraid. He patted him on the back and said, "Let's stop. We need to look around."

The sabertooth was glad to stop and get the boy off his back. He paced nervously as Cai glanced around the village. They were close to the brick building in the center of town where most of the yellow smoke and sulfur fumes were coming from. Cai headed in that direction.

The sulfur odor wasn't bothering Cai as much as it had before. Like Redstripe's fur, he was getting used to it. But he wasn't used to the town being empty. Maybe they were all away at a festival or something.

The boy walked around the brick building, looking for a door. If this was like the mineral baths in Thermala, he assumed that anyone would be welcome to go inside. But when he found the door, he also found that it was locked with a heavy padlock.

"That's weird," said Cai. "You don't see many locks on Dinotopia."

Behind him, Redstripe grumbled nervously. The roof of the building was at least twenty feet over their heads. There was no way to get inside except for the locked door.

Cai was about to walk away and explore someplace else when he heard a shuffling sound. He looked up, thinking the sound was on the roof. Redstripe heard it, too. He started to back away. But he wasn't fast enough.

A net flew off the roof like a giant bat! With weights tied around its edges, it dropped swiftly and covered Redstripe. The sabertooth roared and snapped at the thick strands, but his teeth were for stabbing, not gnawing. The more he struggled, the more tangled up he got.

"Redstripe!" shouted Cai with alarm. "Don't hurt him! Stop it!"

Someone on the roof pulled the ropes tight, and Redstripe was yanked off his feet. With a tremendous roar, he flew into the air and dangled off the side of the building. He looked like a laundry bag full of dirty clothes.

"He's secure!" shouted a voice from the roof. "We've got him!"

"Let him go!" yelled Cai, pounding his fists on the wall. "What are you doing to him?"

Four men peered over the edge of the roof. One of them had a big red beard, and he stared down at Cai.

"What are *we* doing?" he snapped. "We're protecting ourselves! This cat chased a camel over a cliff and nearly scared an old lady to death."

"Turn him loose!" Cai demanded. "It wasn't him."

"Sorry, we can't do that," said the man with the

bushy beard. "Breaking the Oath of Peace is serious. We have to get to the bottom of this."

As Redstripe swung in the wind, he turned his sad yellow eyes toward Cai. The boy reached out to his friend, but he was too high up. Against the thick ropes of the net, both he and Redstripe were helpless.

"I'm sorry," said Cai with tears in his eyes.

The sabertooth let out a roar that shook the snow off the rooftops of Sulfur Springs.

CHAPTER 10

The residents of Sulfur Springs began to come out of their houses to stare at the captured sabertooth. Woolly mammoths, sloths, camels, other mammals, and humans all peered cautiously out of sheds and barns. Cai couldn't believe it—the whole town was afraid of Redstripe!

"You're making a mistake!" he wailed. "He hasn't done anything wrong!"

The man with the red beard threw a ladder off the roof and climbed down. He pointed up to his companions. "Make sure those ropes are tight! We can't let him get away."

Cai marched up to the angry man. "You're right— there *is* a sabertooth causing trouble—but it's not this sabertooth. It's another one, named Neckbiter!"

"I wish it were true," said the man. "But no sabertooth has ever come into the village before. It's too hard to believe that now there are *two* of them prowling around. Where's the other one?"

Cai heaved his skinny shoulders. "I don't know,"

he said unhappily. "We were following Neckbiter. I mean, we didn't know he was coming here, but we had to come here, anyway. Believe me, we know this is a serious threat to the peace of Dinotopia."

The bearded man narrowed his eyes. "Tell me about this Neckbiter."

Cai took a nervous gulp. "Well, first of all, there's an avalanche at Claw Pass. The sabertooths are starving, so he really *is* hungry.

"But Neckbiter is also not at peace with those beyond Sabertooth Mountain. Many years ago, the inhabitants of the mountain, including the sabertooths, were at one with Dinotopia. Then something happened and everyone but the sabertooths left. They've been so separated from us that, with the avalanche in Claw Pass, Neckbiter is trying to convince other sabertooths they should hunt any prey they want."

"Wait a minute," growled the man. "You were traveling with two sabertooth cats, and you *knew* one of them was crazy. Yet you still brought them here without warning us!"

"No," said Cai, shaking his head. "Neckbiter went ahead of us, and he chased the camel here."

Before Cai could explain, a woman shook her fists at him. "Why did you come here? We never did anything to the sabertooths! Why hurt a harmless old woman?"

"She'll be all right," said the man with the red beard. "But the camel is dead."

"It wasn't Redstripe!" Cai insisted. "He has honored his Oath of Peace. He's a civilized Dinotopian, just like any of you."

By now, a large crowd had gathered around. Cai could see their fear, but he also saw their pity and confusion. He knew the pity was as cruel to the proud Redstripe as a beating would be.

The denizens of Sulfur Springs shook their heads and whispered to each other. Cai cringed at the words he overheard.

"The cat has not sought peace."

"He is a lost creature."

"What are we to do with him?"

"There is no place for such a one here. It is not safe."

"He is to be pitied for his insanity. But can we save him from himself?"

"It is a terrible thing for one to have fallen so far."

One by one the people turned away, unable to answer their own questions of how to fit a wild sabertooth into their life.

Cai could only look at Redstripe, who was still tied in the net like a sack of flour. The big cat stared at him, the yellow eyes filled with disappointment and a sorrow of their own. Cai felt the sorrow, too, and a growing sense of betrayal. He hadn't lied to Redstripe! The Dinotopians he knew were kind and generous, but these folks were afraid. And their fear made them blind and closed and inflexible.

"He's innocent!" cried Cai. "Redstripe was only trying to help sabertooths who are starving! He wanted to be *friends,* not enemies. He wanted your help, not nets. He has a family and friends and a home that is in danger. How can you do this?"

The bearded man shrugged his shoulders. "I'm sorry, but we'll have to hold him. The camel is dead, and the old lady had a heart attack. She's now asleep, and our healers think she will be well. When she wakes, maybe she can tell us if your friend is the sabertooth she saw. Until then, we'll have to hold him. For the sake of all."

Cai shook his head. He turned toward Redstripe, but the cat was curled in a ball, his back to the villagers.

"You won't stay a prisoner!" Cai promised his friend as a gentle hand pulled him away.

"I'm Seth, four mothers Icelandic," said the bearded man. "Who might you be?"

"Cai Rochelle, from Thermala."

Seth blinked at him. "Your sister is our Habitat Partner?"

"Yes! Now will you believe me?"

"We won't hurt Redstripe, I promise. In fact, we'll put him someplace where he'll be more comfortable, and give him food."

"But he cannot be held for long," said Cai, tears welling back up. All his feelings about the mountains and his own sense of belonging came back to him.

They mixed together with his new understanding of the sabertooths as well as the things that he had learned about himself.

He gulped and tried to explain. "He's wild, not in a bad way, but in an *alive* way. You don't understand. Being locked up and pitied—it will make him crazy. He needs the mountains and freedom."

Seth guided Cai away from the brick tower. "I'm sure we can clear this up, one way or another. Do you understand why we have to hold the sabertooth?"

Cai let himself be steered away, but he was not about to stop arguing. "And what about the avalanche in Claw Pass? You do have to help the sabertooths. They're really starving."

"Yes, we know all about the avalanche. Moraine and Bigtusk were here until yesterday, but they had to return to the Death Caravan. The wolves are the only ones benefiting from this situation."

Cai's knees began to buckle. He stumbled in the snow. Seth caught him and held him up. "There, lad, you should have some food and rest. My wife, Krihla, has barley soup and cinnamon tea simmering on the stove. We live nearby, so come home with me. Then we'll go to Jasper's funeral."

The boy stared at the man. The words sank in for the first time. It was true—the camel had died. These people had good reason to be afraid of a sabertooth. But they were wrong about which one! If Cai wanted to help Redstripe, he would have to bide his time. He just hoped that Redstripe would be okay until then.

"I suppose," said Cai. He tried not to sound interested, but his stomach growled loudly enough for the neighbors to hear.

He followed the bearded man through the village, ignoring the residents who stared at him and whispered. He was a celebrity—the boy who had fallen from a sky galley, lived to tell about it, then led a murderous sabertooth into their village. They wouldn't forget him for a long while.

"When are Moraine and Bigtusk coming back?" he asked.

Seth shrugged. "Who knows? They could gallop into town at any moment, or not for days. We know they're at the crossroads of the Bison and Mammoth trails. We sent a messenger to find them. Believe me, news of your return, plus a sabertooth on the loose, is bound to bring the Habitat Partners running."

Seth ushered him to a nearby cottage. There was a round table in the front room and Seth pulled out a chair for Cai. Cai sat down and Seth disappeared into the next room. A sloth poked his head in one of the windows to get a look at Cai, who tried to ignore him.

Seth returned with a bowl of hearty soup. Cai wolfed it down. After two more bowls, strength was returning to his limbs. He nearly felt normal. Nearly.

Cai took a deep breath. "Can I please visit Redstripe now?"

Seth scratched his beard and looked hard at the

boy. "I guess so. You won't like it when you see where we've put him—it's called the pit. But it's safe, and we have no prisons or such."

Cai's jaw tightened. "How bad is this pit?"

"It used to be an artesian well before it ran dry one day. Then we plugged it up and used it for storage. There's heat at the bottom, because it's near a sulfur vent. So your friend won't freeze to death. If he's used to caves, this should be no worse."

Except that he can't *go* anywhere, Cai thought.

"Do you think you can walk?" Seth asked, his voice breaking through Cai's thoughts.

Cai set his last bowl of soup aside and stood up. His legs were wobbly, but they didn't buckle. He looked at Seth and nodded. "I'm ready to go."

"Okay, lad. Just remember that the pit is temporary. We hope to resolve this before much longer."

Cai tried not to show how scared and angry he was. There was no point in getting the residents of Sulfur Springs mad at him. And there were good reasons to stay friendly with them. Cai didn't want to be watched all the time himself. If he was going to help Redstripe, he had to keep as cool as morning frost.

They walked past the brick building, which was spewing yellow fog. Now that he was thinking calmly, Cai realized that the building was not a public bath but a power station that used thermal energy to generate electricity.

They turned down a side street where artisans and

craftspeople were working in tiny stalls. Some of them were pounding glowing bars into hinges and nails; others were firing clay cups in hot kilns. A few were carving wood.

One old man was making a beautiful stained-glass window out of lead and colored glass. He waved to them as they strolled past. "I'm thinking about putting a sabertooth cat in my picture, but I'm not sure how."

Cai and Seth stopped to look at the complex scene that the artisan had made, of bison leaping across a gorge.

"A sabertooth could be leaping after the bison," suggested Seth.

"No," said Cai. "A sabertooth wouldn't be hunting anything. They have all taken the Oath of Peace. Unless you want to show a sabertooth that's been driven mad, or how about one that's hanging upside down in a net? That's the only way *you've* ever even seen a sabertooth."

The artisan frowned. "I'll think I'll just leave the sabertooth out."

"Good idea," grumbled Seth. He guided Cai away from the stalls and toward a crowd of Dinotopians at the end of what looked like an alley.

Cai's stomach twisted into more knots as they went through the crowd. He ignored the people and mammals who stared at him as he made his way to the edge of the pit. Maybe they thought he was like Neckbiter, too. With a lump sticking in his throat, Cai peered over the edge into the darkness.

It was indeed a pit—dark, dank, and deep. There seemed to be nothing at the bottom but the smell of old onions and black, loamy earth.

"Redstripe!" shouted Cai with alarm.

A tawny shape stalked into a beam of light in the corner of the pit. The sabertooth didn't look hurt. It was a relief to see him walking around. He growled wearily and stalked back into the shadows.

"He doesn't seem glad to see you," Seth observed.

Cai's shoulders slumped. "Of course not. He blames *me* for telling him that he could trust people, that we would help feed his starving cubs. It just shows that I don't even know my own kind."

"Well, we didn't do anything either," muttered Seth. "Why did we have to get attacked by a psychotic sabertooth?"

"Just bad luck, on both our parts." Cai had no better answer. He got down on his stomach and gazed into the grim pit. He could smell Redstripe's fur mixed with the odors of sulfur and steam.

"Careful there!" shouted Seth. "He can jump real high."

Cai ignored the warning as he pressed his hand into the soft mud at the top of the pit. He pressed four letters into the mud that spelled "Wait."

Redstripe's bright eyes glimmered in the darkness. Before Cai could write more, strong hands pulled him away from the edge.

"You're still touched in the head," growled Seth. "You stay away from that cat. He is not in his right mind. Truthfully, I have no idea what we're going to do with him. We've never had this happen before. There are no records to help us."

Cai could sense the man's frustration with the situation, but it was hard to feel sympathy when he looked at the pit. Instead, he just tried to take care of the things he could.

"Are you feeding Redstripe and giving him water?" he asked.

"We lowered down a bucket of water, but he knocked it over. We don't know what to feed him. Does he eat anything other than meat?"

"No," said Cai. "But he didn't choose to be a meat eater, you know—he was born that way."

Suddenly, Cai caught sight of a tall sapling with very few branches on it that grew close to the far edge of the pit. If he had an ax or a saw, it would only take a few chops to fell the tree. He could push the top into the hole and let Redstripe climb out. His mind whirred while he nodded at the flow of apologies and protests that came from Seth's lips.

Cai's stomach gave a lurch at the thought of helping Redstripe escape. He did understand the dilemma of the villagers. But he also understood the proud sabertooth. Cai knew that what he'd told Seth was true: Redstripe really wouldn't last long in captivity. And Cai knew he would soon try to fight his way out if there was no other option. It was considerably more dangerous for everyone to keep Redstripe down there than to let him go.

Seth stopped talking and gave Cai a funny look. "What are you thinking about?"

"Nothing," said Cai. He pretended to yawn. "All I can think about is how tired I am. Could I go back to your place and lie down?"

"Sure," answered Seth with a friendly smile. "That's the first sensible thing you've said all day. You rest for a while. Then we'll go to the funeral."

Cai walked slowly as they made their way past the craft stalls. He tried not to look too curious as he studied the goods of every potter, woodworker, and metalworker. He didn't see what he was looking for until they came to the very last stall. There a woodworker was fitting new handles onto old tools.

Inside the booth Cai saw picks, shovels, hammers, and various farm implements. Then he stopped short and took a deep breath. At the end of a row of hoes was a heavy ax for chopping wood. The boy looked around to make sure that Seth hadn't noticed his sudden interest in tools, but the man was talking to a friend.

Now all Cai had to do was wait until dark.

CHAPTER 11

The long-necked camels stood solemnly in line at Jasper's funeral. They bleated and sniffled as Jasper's mortal remains were lowered into a bubbling pit of lye. His cleansed bones would be placed in a special box called an ossuary for his family and friends to cherish always.

In addition to the camels, the funeral was attended by humans, mastodons, sloths, and other giant mammals. Cai kept looking around for Marcus, hoping the miner would show up for his friend's funeral. But he was apparently still hiding out.

The old woman remained unconscious and thus unable to clear Redstripe's name. But who knew how much she would remember about the sabertooth who had surprised her, anyway? There was no question about it, Cai decided. He and Redstripe had to get away before they got blamed for anything else.

Cai folded his hands in front of him and tried to look as somber as the other mourners. He glanced up at the sky. Another night was rapidly approaching.

How many nights had he spent outdoors in the wilderness since leaving the Tentpole of the Sky? There were so many that it was beginning to seem normal. He wasn't even sure that he *could* sleep indoors anymore.

Cai shook his head in wonder. He couldn't believe that this was him, Cai Rochelle, thinking about leaving a perfectly good village to spend *more* nights in the mountains. Worse yet, he planned to turn against the villagers to help a predator suspected of the worst crime, murder—albeit unjustly. Things were upside down, but there was nothing he could do about it.

As the funeral ended, people and mammals broke up into small groups and talked quietly. Cai planned his next move. No one was paying much attention to him. Even Seth had his back to him.

Cai figured he might have five or ten minutes before they realized he was gone. Smiling and nodding, he backed slowly through the crowd of people, careful not to draw attention to himself. Finally, he stepped out from under the natural archway that protected the lye baths.

Above, a few clouds covered the crescent of moon, and stars winked on the edges of the sky. The darkness helped to cover his escape. Cai was soon running full speed to the thermal power plant in the center of town, which was the only way he knew how to find the artisans' street. He ran past the brick building and down the narrow side street. As he had hoped, most of the stalls were closed, although a few scattered lights showed craftspeople still working.

The walls of the stalls were nothing more than a few canvas tarps tied to the ground. Cai figured he could crawl under the canvas. First he had to find the stall he wanted—the one where he had seen the ax. Cai found a stall that seemed to be in the right location, but he didn't know for sure. Holding his breath, he got down on the frozen mud and crawled under the canvas flap.

It was pitch-black inside the stall. All Cai wanted to do was get his hands on the ax and get out. Blindly, he felt around in the darkness. His hands wandered over tools of all sorts that were on a high table, but the ax was not among them. Well, at least he knew he was in the right place. Cai moved to feel for another worktable. Instead, he bumped right into a pile of table legs, which fell to the ground with a terrific clatter.

Cai froze and held his breath until he was sure that no one was coming to investigate. Slowly his eyes were adjusting to the darkness. He found another stack of old tools. Then his breath caught in his throat. There was the ax, lying alone on a low bench.

The boy wrapped his fingers around the ax and hugged it to his chest. He fought the temptation to think of it as a weapon; it was a tool, and he would use it as such. Cai felt bad about having to steal an ax and kill a tree, but these were desperate times. He would leave the ax behind for its rightful owner.

Next he had to get to the pit. Knowing he didn't have much time, Cai crouched down and ran along the alley behind the stalls. He heard distant voices, but almost everyone in town was still at Jasper's funeral. His luck held until he got to the pit.

There were two guards standing next to the ugly hole in the ground. Cai ducked out of sight behind a tree. One of the guards was eating his dinner, but the other was pacing nervously. He kept gazing into the hole at the very quiet sabertooth. The only noise on the chilly but gentle evening was a tinker's hammer.

"He's too silent," said the guard, as if reading Cai's mind. "Just too darn silent."

"Oh, even he deserves a rest," said the other man as he gobbled down a big biscuit. "After all, we gave him some of Jasper—peace be with him—so he shouldn't be hungry. You know, I'm really not so sure we got ourselves the right sabertooth."

"That's okay," said the worried guard. "I feel better knowing he's down there rather than walking around on the streets."

Cai looked over his shoulder. He expected Seth to come charging down the alley at any moment, sounding an alarm. He had to get the guards away from that pit, but how? He needed a distraction, and he needed it now.

The boy had heard enough sabertooth growls to know just what they sounded like. He scrambled into the nearest stall and began to bang around the pots, pans, and tools, making a terrific noise. Then he roared like a sabertooth for all he was worth. Cai roared until his throat was sore.

When he heard the shouts, he rolled onto his back and slipped quietly out the rear of the stall. The two guards were cautiously approaching the suddenly silent booth. Cai waited until they were right next to it, then he jumped to his feet.

"Sabertooth! Sabertooth!" he shouted, pointing up the alley, away from the pit. "He ran that way! Get him!"

Cai was staying out of sight. He wanted the guards to think that he had run for it, while he sneaked away on his hands and knees. He was heading for the far side of the pit where the slender tree he had spotted earlier stood. He was careful not to bang the ax on anything and make a noise.

The guards were frozen, unable to decide whether to stay with the sabertooth they had or to go try and catch the sabertooth that was on the loose. Cai held his breath and waited. Finally, he got a break when one of the artisans shrieked and knocked over some goods in his stall. The two guards immediately rushed to the opposite end of the street. As soon as they did, Cai jumped to his feet and dashed toward the tree.

As he went around the edge of the pit, Cai looked down. Redstripe was pacing tensely. The cat didn't growl or jump up—he was being patient, as Cai had told him to be. For the moment, the sabertooth was waiting to see what the boy had in mind.

Cai wasn't big and muscular, but he had chopped fallen logs before. He staggered up to the sapling and swung the ax as hard as he could. The tree trunk was slender, but it had thick bark. The ax stuck, and he couldn't pull it out! As Cai yanked and yanked on the handle, he heard dozens of angry voices behind him.

"There he is! There he is!"

"He's got an ax!"

"It's an escape!"

"Stop right there!" bellowed Seth over the other voices.

Instead of stopping, the fear gave Cai a jolt of strength. He yanked the ax out of the tree and made a short downward chop, followed by a quick upward one. As he had learned, he was making a V in the side of the tree.

Redstripe growled encouragement—or maybe it was a warning that the angry villagers were getting closer. Cai glanced up to see Seth leading a dozen men, plus a woolly rhino! The boy swung the ax like a mighty scythe!

The sapling cracked and began to give way. Cai barely had time to reach up and pull the splintered trunk toward the pit. The woolly rhino thundered to a stop at the edge of the hole. Cai threw all his weight onto the tree and pushed the top of it deep into the pit.

A flash of fur and sinewy muscle rose out of the

darkness and landed on the branches. The trunk jerked out of Cai's hands, and he fell backward. Redstripe was a blur of motion as he clawed his way up the tree trunk, until with a final tremendous leap he landed in the soft mud on the edge of the pit and roared like a volcano.

"Hooray!" shouted Cai, shoving his fist in the air.

There wasn't much time to savor the escape. The woolly rhino came charging around one side of the pit, and Seth came chugging around the other. Cai shrank back, knowing that this was Redstripe's department.

As the rhino thundered toward him, the sabertooth leaped high in the air with his back arched. He landed on the rhino's flanks and sank his claws into several tender spots. The rhino honked with shock and spun around like a lopsided top. Redstripe barely got out of the way as the huge beast crashed into Seth and knocked him on his back!

The sight of the frightened rhino stopped most of the villagers in their tracks. Cai took that moment to leap up on Redstripe's back. Cai gripped the sabertooth's neck as they bounded through the alley and down the main street. They jumped over the last line of people who stood blocking their way at the edge of the village. As Redstripe flew over their heads, they screamed and threw themselves to the ground.

A few villagers picked themselves up and gave chase, but Redstripe and Cai had a good lead and were faster. Soon they had left the village far behind.

Hours later, the sabertooth slowed to a weary walk, and Cai finally let go of his neck. Overhead the gloomy clouds of night were curled around the jagged peaks of the Forbidden Mountains.

"It's just me and you," said Cai glumly. "We're miles away from Sabertooth Mountain, and nobody will help us."

Redstripe looked at Cai with a stern expression and curled his lip. Cai had learned that the great cat did not feel sorry for himself, unlike a foolish boy who didn't know when he had it good. The sabertooth accepted the twists and turns of his chaotic life, sometimes with anger but always with action.

Cai wanted to be more like Redstripe, more accepting of small things he couldn't change, like being at the Tentpole of the Sky. If he had learned anything in the last few days, it was that being alive and free in the outdoors was enough to make him happy.

He hugged Redstripe's neck and felt the sabertooth begin to purr. As long as they had each other, they could lick any problem. He just wished there weren't so many problems facing them, including the fact that they were lost. At the very least, this was not the way they had entered Sulfur Springs. It was hard to tell if they were even on a proper trail.

Most important, they still had to worry about Neckbiter. Where had the dark-furred cat disappeared to? He had wanted to cause trouble, and he had succeeded—hundreds of villagers were upset. Neckbiter might return home, thought Cai, to bring more of his followers through Claw Pass. That's where they should look for him.

Also, the boy couldn't forget about Seth and the rest of that crowd. They were scared now, but in the morning they would be angry, and feeling braver. There were lots of camels and mammoths in that village who knew this region better than Cai and Redstripe. They could be tracked, even with the fresh snow.

Cai patted Redstripe's back until he slowed down, then the boy jumped off. He wanted to give the cat a break, because he had to be suffering from those long hours spent in that awful pit. If only they had a compass, thought Cai, they could strike out toward Sky City, or even Thermala.

Redstripe stopped suddenly and growled. Cai couldn't see anything but gloomy buttes and bottomless gorges all around them. Then shadows moved to his right, and Cai jumped. Redstripe lowered his head and growled. It was a deep, threatening sound. More shapes moved behind them, reaching outward like lengthening shadows at sunset. Cai stared at the dark shapes skulking toward them, and he finally realized what they were:

Dire wolves!

There must have been twenty or thirty of them, a big pack of ferocious wolves. Redstripe roared a warning to the wolves, but they didn't stop. A gray wolf prowled the rear, barking orders, and the wolves circled slowly around Cai and Redstripe. The circle pinched tighter.

The sabertooth looked at Cai and growled. The boy jumped up on his back, and they bounded over the first rank of wolves. Half a dozen more nipped at Redstripe's legs. The sabertooth finally stumbled, and Cai was tossed over his shoulders into a snowbank.

The lad sputtered and sat up. He saw Redstripe whirl around and leap at the nearest wolf. The creature went down instantly, but more dire wolves were creeping up behind them.

In their low growls and cool eyes, Cai could almost read the wolves' thoughts: *This is our territory, and sabertooths are not welcome to come here and cause problems.*

Redstripe growled and slashed at their snouts with his claws, but he couldn't guard every direction. Cai watched helplessly as the large pack of wolves closed in on the lone sabertooth.

CHAPTER 12

"Help!" yelled Cai.

A wolf turned toward him and wheezed with laughter. Who was going to hear a boy's pathetic cry for help way out here? The wolves were much more concerned about the claws and teeth of the ferocious sabertooth. They could ignore Cai until they were finished with Redstripe.

"Get away from him!" shouted Cai. "Help! Help!"

One wolf suddenly had had enough of the noisy human and leaped upon his chest. Cai was knocked onto his back, and he opened his eyes to see a long snout full of teeth snapping and snarling in his face.

Cai punched the wolf with his elbow, and the animal narrowed his eyes and drew back his lips. He was about to bite Cai when the boy felt the ground thundering beneath him. At first he thought it was a sulfur vent, until he heard the angry trumpet of a woolly mammoth.

The wolf on his chest looked up just as two huge tusks slid under his belly, picked him up, and pushed him away like a furry pillow. Cai scurried out of the way as the mammoth trumpeted and stomped the ground.

The mammoth next turned his attention to the wolves who were attacking Redstripe. He charged into the fray and flailed his mighty tusks, throwing wolves left and right. The ground trembled as the mammoth spun around and smashed a new wave of attackers. With frightened yelps, the wolves scrambled all over each other to escape. Redstripe snapped at their heels to hurry them along.

When it was all over, the sabertooth and the woolly mammoth stood side by side, huffing and puffing. Cai ran over and hugged Redstripe. The big cat had scratches all over his body, but he didn't seem to be badly hurt.

Cai and Redstripe looked warily at the mammoth, wondering what he would do next. When mammoths got mad, they could be dangerous to everybody around them.

"Aren't you tired of getting into trouble?" came a weary voice from behind them.

Cai whirled around to see Moraine striding toward them across the snow. He looked back at the mammoth and realized that it was Bigtusk. Cai hadn't recognized the mammoth in the dark. His heart sank.

Moraine and Bigtusk would be harder to get rid of than a pack of wolves.

Cai gently rubbed Redstripe's fur. "Thanks for

your help. But we have to be going now."

The tall, dark-haired woman stopped and crossed her arms. "Wait a minute, Little Brother. I tracked you by coming through Sulfur Springs, so I know what you've been up to. We've got to go back to the village—those people have some questions for you. Then Mom and Dad might want to see you, too."

"No!" Cai hugged Redstripe tightly. "They trapped him in a net and threw him into a pit! And they blamed him for something another cat did. Somebody has got to believe me. I've been with Redstripe every minute for days. He didn't hurt anyone."

Cai pointed to the stark mountains behind them. "You know about the avalanche—you know how serious it is. I've been in their caves. I've seen the cubs that have to be fed. Unless we can stop this other sabertooth, there will be more trouble. Redstripe came to them as a friend, and they attacked him."

Moraine looked warily at the banged-up sabertooth, and Redstripe stared back. The cat moved a bit closer to Cai, as if he would protect him from this ferocious woman. Moraine looked at Bigtusk, and the mammoth gave her a mammoth shrug. She found a rock, brushed off the snow, and sat down.

"Okay," said Moraine. "Why don't you tell me everything you've been doing since your quick exit from the sky galley."

Cai told Moraine and Bigtusk about falling into the snowdrift, his scary meeting with Redstripe, and his even scarier meeting with Neckbiter. The cave, the council of sabertooths in the ancient hall, and the old scrolls—he told her about all of it.

He told her how Killer and Slash had helped them escape through Claw Pass, plus the second time that Redstripe saved his life. Moraine stared wide-eyed as he told her about the journey through the bear caves, the meeting with the mother bear, and the graveyard of great mammals in the snow and ice.

"Neckbiter passed us in the cave," Cai explained. "That's how he got ahead of us."

Moraine nodded. "Yes, but there's no proof of that. The villagers have only seen *one* sabertooth. Unfortunately, that's Redstripe."

"That's not true," said Cai. "There's a quartz miner, Marcus, who can clear this up. He was attacked by Neckbiter and got away from him."

"Where is this Marcus?" asked Moraine.

"Still on Bison Trail," answered Cai, "camped on a ledge. He's between Rhino Rock and Claw Pass."

Moraine stood up and slapped her thighs. "Okay, let's move out. We've got enough light to walk, and I know a shortcut to Rhino Rock."

She pointed to Redstripe. "He's a little banged up, so maybe you would prefer to ride with me on Bigtusk."

Cai scratched Redstripe's head. "Thanks, I'll do that."

Moraine gave the boy a smile. "When they told

me you were riding a sabertooth, I could hardly believe it. Making friends with Redstripe is a big breakthrough. I'm proud of you, Cai."

"Thanks."

"But no more stealing axes, chopping down trees, and causing an uproar."

"I'll be very happy to have a peaceful life after this," Cai assured her.

Cai climbed up on the woolly mammoth, behind Moraine. Thanks to Bigtusk's gentle rocking motion, he fell asleep as they rode along. His head rested on Moraine's back, and she smiled fondly at the weight.

Cai was amazed when he woke up and saw the first rays of sun reaching the mountains to the east like fingers. One of them was Sabertooth Mountain, but it was still shrouded in charcoal and pink clouds.

He suddenly realized that his pillow was the hood of Moraine's jacket. Cai bolted upright and mumbled, "Sorry about that."

"I'm glad you got a chance to sleep," said Moraine with a grin. "You'll need your wits about you. Whatever happens, I want you to stay close to me. Is that clear?"

"But Redstripe needs help," said Cai.

"I think Redstripe can take care of himself far better out here than you or I. We're going to find Marcus and go back to town. And there's to be no argument, because we're simply not safe here."

Cai couldn't disagree. He didn't want to see Neck-biter again. But he had an uncomfortable feeling that the dark cat was not far away. A sabertooth growl sounded in the distance. Bigtusk thudded to a stop and held perfectly still. Redstripe growled back.

"Stay close to me," said Moraine. "For the moment, I'm staying right here, on top of Bigtusk."

"Okay," agreed Cai. He stared into the dawn, but he couldn't see anything but rocks, snow, and a few fir trees. Then he saw two sleek shapes, bounding through the drifts and over the gorges.

Cai could feel Bigtusk tensing under his legs. The mammoth was having a hard time holding still.

Moraine rubbed Bigtusk behind his gigantic, hairy ears. "We can't outrun them, so we have to make friends. If my brother did it, then so can we."

"Still," said Cai, "be ready to run."

Bigtusk hooted his trunk and stomped his feet, unable to contain his fear any longer. The sabertooths loped closer and closer. But the nearer they got, the less threatening they looked. In fact, they looked dog-tired, all three of them.

Suddenly, Redstripe bounded forward to meet the two sabertooths as they collapsed with exhaustion. At almost the same moment, Cai gave a happy cry.

"I know them!" he told Moraine. "That's Slash and Killer, the ones I told you about. You have to let me down."

"No," said Moraine. "It's too dangerous."

"Please," said Cai.

There must have been something grown-up in his voice. Moraine turned to look at him and didn't answer for a long moment. Finally, she nodded and leaned over to whisper in Bigtusk's ear. The mammoth knelt down long enough for Cai to jump off, then he rose to his feet and trumpeted a warning.

The sabertooths were too tired to care about the blarings of some mammoth, but they did swarm around Cai. He petted all three of the big cats and told Slash and Killer how glad he was to see them again. He noted that the two sabertooths had new wounds. Slash and Killer had been fighting their own battles.

Cai asked Slash and Killer how they had gotten through the pass.

Slash glanced at Killer, but the old sabertooth was done in. He could hardly lift his chin off the snow long enough to nod to Slash. The female sabertooth started the story by pressing letters into the snow.

The letters spelled "Neckbiter."

Moraine climbed down off Bigtusk and peered over Cai's shoulder at Slash's writing. "My gosh," she said, "they know the dinosaur footprint language!"

"I told you," said Cai. "There was a whole civilization on Sabertooth Mountain with all kinds of Dinotopians, but now only the sabertooths are left."

Moraine frowned in thought. Cai could tell that her opinion of this venture was changing with every second. She had to believe him now, since she saw Neckbiter's name written in paw prints in the snow.

Unfortunately, the story that Slash reported was very grim. Neckbiter had returned and gathered more followers. Fearing the sabertooths, the bears had cleared out of the caves running through Claw Pass that had allowed most of them to get through the pass underground.

Moraine gazed up at the sky. "I'm hoping for a miracle."

"A storm?" asked Cai.

Moraine shook her head and gazed skyward. "I hope he comes through, but it may be too late. You know, if we were smart, we wouldn't go anywhere near Neckbiter and an army of sabertooths. Shall we turn back to the village?"

"No," answered Cai. "We have to try to reason with him. We've got Redstripe, Slash, and Killer to help us. We don't want to have problems with the sabertooths in the future."

"All right." Moraine waved to Bigtusk and made a motion with her hands. "I'll walk with you and the sabertooths. I want to leave Bigtusk free to defend us if need be."

"Okay." Cai lowered his head. "Have you seen Mom and Dad yet?"

"No, but I sent them a message. They think you're dead, so it would be a nice surprise for them if you lived through this."

"It would be a nice surprise for *me*," muttered Cai.

The sabertooths picked themselves up and began the long walk back toward Claw Pass. Cai and Moraine followed them on foot, and the mammoth brought up the rear, making worried snorts. Bigtusk looked ready to trample anyone who threatened his partner.

After they passed Rhino Rock, Moraine motioned toward a snow-capped ledge some distance away. "I see a sentinel up there," she whispered to Cai. "Neckbiter must have sent his followers scouting ahead. We've been spotted."

"We'll meet them soon," agreed Cai.

They trudged through a hollow that was swamped with snow and were just climbing out of it when they heard the roars. Redstripe, Slash, and Killer fell back, guarding the humans, and Bigtusk snorted nervously.

Cai watched in awe as a parade of giant cats came over the rise. There were old cats, cubs, pregnant cats—whole prides of sabertooths—with Neckbiter in the lead. The dark-furred cat looked very satisfied with his newfound stature.

Moraine scowled. "Most of them look hungry, and that's not good."

The mighty cats growled and roared in unison at the intruders. Cai was stricken with fear. More than anything, he wanted to get back on top of Bigtusk and run for it. The roars of all the hungry cats were chilling—they were a chorus of death.

Moraine glanced at him. He could tell that she didn't know what to do either. They fell back closer to Bigtusk, and Killer and Slash fell back closer to them. Redstripe bounded forward to cut off Neckbiter. He met the dark-furred cat at the top of the rise, and they stood silhouetted in a patch of sunlight.

Out of nowhere, two sabertooths jumped on Redstripe from behind and wrestled him to the ground. Neckbiter spun around and headed straight toward Cai and Moraine.

Bigtusk swung his tusks and knocked away a sabertooth who was sneaking up behind them. Slash and Killer roared in their defense, but a hundred sabertooth cats closed in from all around.

CHAPTER 13

His jaws wide open, teeth pointed out like bayonets, Neckbiter bore down on Cai and Moraine. The humans froze. Everything was a blur, except for Neckbiter leaping through the air, teeth first!

Before Cai closed his eyes, there was a flash to his left, and a tan body hit Neckbiter in the stomach. It was Slash, and she knocked the murderous sabertooth just inches away from Cai. The two cats wrestled in the snow, and Slash got on top and sliced downward with her canine teeth.

She clipped Neckbiter in the shoulder, and the dark cat hissed and leaped away. He didn't have to fight alone, as he had many hungry friends. The giant cats crept closer, snarling and flashing their teeth.

Killer and Slash jumped to Cai's side and growled at the others, but they were quickly surrounded by enemies. The boy looked for Redstripe, but he was nowhere to be found. Four sabertooths jumped on Bigtusk's back, but the mammoth whirled around and tossed them off.

Snarling and snapping, the hungry sabertooths closed in. Cai knew he had to do something, but what? He suddenly remembered that he knew how to roar, so he cut loose with a roar like the one he had used at the pit. He roared until his throat was raw, getting every sabertooth's attention.

Once Cai got the cats' attention, he reached down and hugged Killer and Slash. The sight of the roaring boy hugging two sabertooths must have stirred some memory in the pride. It was like one of the murals in the ancient hall. Neckbiter roared, urging his followers to attack, but they came no closer.

The cloud cover broke overhead, and Cai felt the warmth of the sun. He looked up to see a sky galley sailing into view!

The boy grabbed Slash's shoulder and pointed up. "Look at that! This is becoming a regular stop on the sky galley cruises."

Moraine shielded her eyes from the sun and looked upward. "Could it be?" she asked excitedly. She jumped around and waved. "Down here! Down here!"

The sabertooths stared at this behavior, but nobody was going to argue with a crazy human. The cats paced nervously and hissed as the sky galley swooped ever lower. Finally, it hovered in place. The galleymaster leaned over the railing and waved.

Cai gasped at the familiar face of Ramón. "Hello to the ground!" Ramón yelled. "Moraine, I have your cargo! Would this be a good place for it?"

"Yes, I think so. Drop it here!" Moraine brushed her long black hair off her face, and she was beaming with happiness.

"Heads up!" shouted Ramón.

Then the huge doors in the underbelly of the ship dropped open. Tons of silvery objects floated out of the cargo hatch. At first, Cai thought they were silver bars, or knives, until a fat mackerel hit him in the face.

He gazed up in amazement to see it was raining fish! Plump groupers and skinny eels, long sea bass and short sardines—fish poured from the sky and covered the snow. Moraine roared with laughter.

At first, the sabertooths fled, except for the little ones, who were too hungry to be afraid. The cubs were the first to attack the mackerel and bass, ripping out big chunks with their little canines. One by one, the adults came forward and tried the delicacies. Most of them had never seen fish before, thought Cai, surely not an abundance like this. Like most cats, they didn't need long to discover they liked this new food.

Cai could see Killer, Slash, and even Neckbiter eating gratefully, but he couldn't find Redstripe. Then he remembered that the cat had been attacked up on the ridge, and Cai hadn't seen him since then.

Worried, Cai dashed up the hill to find his friend. The sabertooths parted and let him through. He finally found Redstripe, lying wounded on the ground.

Three sabertooths were guarding him, and they didn't want to let Cai get near.

Redstripe growled, and they stepped aside to let the boy pass. Fighting back tears, Cai rushed forward and held Redstripe. His scratches from before looked like nothing compared to these wounds. Cai could tell that the sabertooth had lost a lot of blood.

He hugged the big cat. "Look, they're all eating! Your pride isn't hungry anymore! Come on, Redstripe. Please don't die."

The sabertooth growled weakly, and Cai heard footsteps behind him. He turned to see Moraine and Bigtusk rushing toward him. Tearfully, Cai looked up at the Habitat Partners. "He's not going to die, is he?"

Moraine rolled up her sleeves. "I've got lots of medicines in my pack. He's not going to die if I can help it."

"Whoopee!" shouted a distant voice. "I've got some aloe vera salve!"

Cai looked up to see Marcus standing at the top of a pinnacle. It must have taken the miner hours to get up there, but he had had a great view of the amazing events in the hollow.

"Get down here!" ordered Moraine. "And bring any medicines you have with you!"

One month later, Cai sat on the floor of the great hall beneath Sabertooth Mountain. He gazed at the domed ceiling, the giant pillars, the box of scrolls, and the paintings of humans and sabertooths. The boy ruffled the fur on the back of Redstripe, who was sitting beside him.

Redstripe still wore a few bandages, and he wasn't up to his full strength yet. But he was alive. Even better, the avalanche had mostly melted, and sick and dying mammals were again making the sacred journey to Claw Pass. Once again the sabertooths had plenty to eat, and life was back to normal. Only one thing was different: the thirteen-year-old boy who was living with them.

Cai knew he couldn't stay much longer, not with the pass open. Redstripe was almost well, and Moraine had started giving the boy impatient looks. Soon it would be time for them to move on, but Cai didn't want to leave Sabertooth Mountain. This seemed like home to him now.

But he had another life—parents, friends, and school. Maybe he would even give the Tentpole of the Sky another try. The things he had learned there had served him well on his adventure.

Cai knew he could leave this majestic hall, Sabertooth Mountain, and the mammal graveyard, but he didn't know if he could leave Redstripe. But there was no way the cat could go with him. As leader of his pride, Redstripe had responsibilities here.

Cai heard footsteps in one of the tunnels that led into the vast hall. He turned around, expecting to see

Moraine, and he wasn't disappointed. Redstripe growled in greeting. Ever since Moraine had patched him up, they had been great friends. Sometimes it made Cai jealous.

Moraine stood in the doorway, smiling. "You have some visitors."

"Me?" Cai asked in disbelief.

Moraine nodded.

Cai jumped to his feet. "Really? Up here?"

Moraine stepped aside, and several people entered the hall.

The first two in cried out Cai's name and held out their arms.

"Mom! Dad!" The boy ran to hug his parents, and soon the whole family, including Moraine, was laughing with joy.

"What are you doing here?" he asked. "I was coming back to you."

"No need," said his father. "We've been given the job of surveying the ruins down here, the ones *you* discovered. We meet tomorrow with the Sabertooth Council. We were just waiting until the snow melted to join you. It's a big job—I figure we'll be here a year."

"A year!" cried Cai. He looked in amazement from his parents to Redstripe. "You mean I don't have to leave?"

His mother smiled. "Not for a year. After that,

you can continue your schooling wherever you want. I'm looking forward to seeing spring and summer on this beautiful mountain."

"And there are other people to see you and Redstripe," added Moraine.

Cai was so excited about seeing his parents that he hadn't noticed the other people. Now he recognized Seth and other folks from the village. The big man with the red beard looked apologetic.

"We were hasty and misjudged your friend," he said. "We have a scroll for Redstripe, recognizing him as an official ambassador to our village. Next time he visits, we'll roll out the red carpet!"

Seth unfolded a beautiful scroll that had golden lettering in the dinosaur language. With a bow and a nervous expression, he presented it to Redstripe. The sabertooth took the scroll in his mouth and set it on the ground. Carefully, he spread it out with his paws and began to read. When he finished, he nodded majestically at the villagers. Their faces broke into smiles and quiet cheers.

"Well," said Seth, "we'll leave you now. But we'll look forward to your visit."

The villagers filed out, pausing to shake hands with Moraine, and to Cai's great surprise, with him as well.

When they'd all left, Cai's father turned to Redstripe. "Our boy wasn't interested in anything until he met you. At your side, he's turned into a man. Thank you."

Redstripe looked at Cai and gave a growl of agreement.

Moraine looked over her happy family.

"Now that everyone's here, I think it's time for Bigtusk and me to be going," said Moraine. "I hear there's a wagon loaded with supplies headed your way."

They all tried to dissuade her, but a Habitat Partner's work is never done. She gave everyone hugs and kisses, including Redstripe. With a big smile, she added, "And don't forget, one year from today there will be a parade in Thermala. It will be in honor of the boy who made friends with the sabertooths."

Redstripe roared his approval, his long teeth glimmering in the light of the crystal caverns.

WINDCHASER
By Scott Ciencin

During a mutiny on a prison ship, two very different boys are tossed overboard and stranded together on the island of Dinotopia. Raymond is the kind-hearted son of the ship's surgeon. He immediately takes to this strange new world of dinosaurs and befriends a wounded Sky-bax named Windchaser. Hugh, on the other hand, is a sly London pickpocket who swears he'll never fit into this paradise.

While Raymond helps Windchaser improve his shaky flying, Hugh forms a sinister plan. Soon all three are headed into a dangerous adventure that will test both their courage and their friendship.

RIVER QUEST
By John Vornholt

Magnolia and Paddlefoot are the youngest pairing of human and dinosaur ever to be made Habitat Partners. Their first mission is to discover what has made the Polongo River dry up and then, an even more difficult task, they must restore it to its usual greatness. Otherwise, Waterfall City, which is powered by energy from the river, is doomed.

Along the way Magnolia and Paddlefoot meet Birch, a farmer's son, and his triceratops buddy, Rogo, who insist on joining the quest. Together, the unlikely four must battle the elements, and sometimes each other, as they undertake a quest that seems nearly impossible.

HATCHLING
By Midori Snyder

Janet is thrilled when she is made an apprentice at the Hatchery, the place where dinosaur eggs are taken care of. But the first time she has to watch over the eggs at night, she falls asleep. When she wakes up, one of the precious dinosaur eggs has a crack in it—a crack that could prove fatal to the baby dinosaur within.

Afraid of what people will think, Janet runs away to find a place where no one knows of her mistake. Instead, she finds Kranog, a wounded hadrosaur. Kranog is trying to return to the abandoned city of her birth to lay her egg, but she can't do it without Janet's help. Now Janet will have to face her fears about both the journey ahead and about herself.

LOST CITY
By Scott Ciencin

In search of adventure, thirteen-year-old Andrew convinces his friends, Lian and Ned, to explore the forbidden Lost City of Dinotopia. But the last thing they expect to discover is a group of meat-eating Troodons!

For centuries, this lost tribe of dinosaurs has lived secretly in the crumbling city. Now Andrew and his friends are trapped. They must talk the tribe into joining the rest of Dinotopia. Otherwise, the Troodons may try to protect their secrets by making Andrew, Ned, and Lian citizens of the Lost City—for good!

THUNDER FALLS

By Scott Ciencin

Coming in November 1996!

Steelgaze, a wise old dinosaur, has become frustrated with his two young charges, Joseph and Fleetfeet. Everything is a contest with these two! Even when Steelgaze sends them on a quest to find a hidden prize possession, Joseph and Fleetfeet turn it into a race against each other. But when they reach the hiding place, they see the prize has been stolen.

Gradually the two track the thief across Dinotopia, but their constant contests are making progress nearly impossible! It's not until they help a shipwrecked girl named Tegan that they finally begin to see the value of cooperating—especially when the three must work together to survive the rapids of Waterfall City's *Thunder Falls!*

REVISIT THE WORLD OF

in these titles,
available wherever books are sold...

OR

You can send in this coupon (with check or money order)
and have the books mailed directly to you!

☐ *Windchaser* (0-679-86981-6) $3.99
by Scott Ciencin

☐ *River Quest* (0-679-86982-4) $3.99
by John Vornholt

☐ *Hatchling* (0-679-86984-0) $3.99
by Midori Snyder

☐ *Lost City* (0-679-86983-2) $3.99
by Scott Ciencin

☐ *Sabertooth Mountain* (0-679-88095-X) $3.99
by John Vornholt

Subtotal . . . . $ _____
Shipping and handling . . . . $ _3.00_
Sales tax (where applicable) . . . . $ _____
Total amount enclosed . . . . $ _____

Name _____

Address _____

City_____State_____Zip _____

Make your check or money order (no cash or C.O.D.s)
payable to Random House and mail to:
Bullseye Mail Sales, 400 Hahn Road, Westminster, MD 21157.

Prices and numbers subject to change without notice. Valid in U.S. only.
All orders subject to availability. Please allow 4 to 6 weeks for delivery.

**Need your books even faster? Call toll-free 1–800–793–2665
to order by phone and use your major credit card.
Please mention interest code 049–20 to expedite your order.**